A Stolen
CALIFORNIA

A NOVEL
BY

DONALD SINCLAIR

authorHOUSE®

AuthorHouse™
1663 Liberty Drive
Bloomington, IN 47403
www.authorhouse.com
Phone: 1 (800) 839-8640

Published by AuthorHouse 01/20/2015

ISBN: 978-1-4969-6552-3 (sc)
ISBN: 978-1-4969-6551-6 (e)

Library of Congress Control Number: 2015900958

Print information available on the last page.

Any people depicted in stock imagery provided by Thinkstock are models, and such images are being used for illustrative purposes only. Certain stock imagery © Thinkstock.

This book is printed on acid-free paper.

CHAPTER 1

Vern Hurley was sitting in Bliss' father's green Buick. Bliss, leaning to look up at Tom, was sitting next to him. They had just driven up to the curb, and parked backwards, the driver side to the curb, where Tom was pushing the lawn mower.

"Look at you," Vern said smiling.

"Yeah," Tom Kemp said, "I'm just home from bumming around Spain. I'll have to live here until I find a job -- on some newspaper."

Vern held up a hand from the car window and they shook hands.

Bliss, leaning over Vern, put her hand out the window to shake hands too, saying, "We flew from California for my brother's wedding -- tomorrow. And while we're here in Detroit, we want to drive up to Montreal to see the Canadian Expo, that's fantastic this year."

"You hear," Vern interrupted, "a race riot broke out today over on the west side -- around 12th Street? It's still going on. Only in Detroit -- things never change."

"Yeah," Tom said looking to the west, "I saw a mountain of black smoke in that direction -- when I was cutting grass in the backyard. A neighbor shouted from the next yard that the rioters were looting and burning stores."

"I hope," Vern said shaking his head, "the riot don't spread over the whole city."

Bliss, pointing to the car radio, said, "they're saying the black smoke is drifting across the expressway -- and they're warning motorists -- to slow down."

"Nah," Tom said, "it won't spread -- when the cops start shooting -- the whole riot will come to a screeching halt."

"Listen," Bliss said, her ear to the radio, "they're looting supermarkets -- and even television shops." Then her mouth dropped open. "The police have been ordered <u>not</u> to shoot -- the reporter says."

"Looks like," Bliss said to Vern, then up at Tom, "we picked a bad time to come home --"
Tom shrugged.

"We didn't know," Vern said quietly, turning, his face almost brushing Bliss' face when she turned her head to hear the car radio.

"I hope the riot," Bliss said thoughtfully, "doesn't interrupt the wedding plans." Her ear was still turned toward the car radio. "We were just on the way to the caterer's -- when we met Mimi Robertson at the gas station -- and she said she saw you at home yesterday, Tom."

"Don't worry, Babe," Vern said to her, watching her face as she sat back in the seat, "the Chicken Kiev will be safe -- the caterer is out here in Harper Woods -- that's a long way from 12th Street."

When she nodded, Tom saw Vern smile, and so she would not see him grinning too, he bent over the lawnmower and began pushing the grass clippings to the rear of the catcher-basket behind the blades.

"Tom," Bliss said in a loud voice, "why don't you come to the wedding? We're inviting you -- aren't we Vern? You can even bring a date -- if you want."

"Yeah, Sluggo," Vern said, "you might get inspired to have a wedding of your own."

"I'll wait and see," Tom said through the open car window, his face down next to the car as he was pushing back the grass clippings.

"There's a lot to do around the house. Mom let a lot of stuff slide around here -- since dad died last spring -- he used to take care of this outside work."

He caught a flash of her round thing when she flipped her skirt above her knees while getting settled in the car seat.

"When are you going to find some nice girl, Tom?" she said smiling. "One that will make you settle down -- quit all this wandering -- trying to be like Hemingway -- wandering to all those foreign countries -- trying to make a living writing stories."

"Hey," Vern said leaning to the dashboard radio, "the rioters are looting <u>all</u> the stores on 12th Street -- and the cops are just standing, not doing anything -- not shooting."

Tom said quietly, "The mayor doesn't want a bloodbath."

"Oh," Bliss said making a face, "you reporters know everything -- don't you smarty?"

She wiggled her hips, grinning at Tom.

"I think we should get going," Vern said. "In case the cops start closing down the roads -- or something."

"I never thought of that," Bliss said putting her hand on Vern's arm.

"We're staying with Bliss' parents," Vern said starting the car engine, looking up at Tom. "Bliss is helping her mom with the wedding preparation stuff. Call me at the house tomorrow. Okay?"

*　　*　　*　　*

At the wedding hall, sitting at a table at the front of the dance floor, the band blaring the song <u>Love Is a Many Splendored Thing</u>, Tom, turning his glass of scotch on the table, said, "Hey, Vern, the radio says the riot's simmering down on 12th Street."

"Yep," Vern said, his eyes glazed from too many scotches, "when President Johnson ordered those paratroopers in from Kentucky -- it was like the cops showing up at the door of some wild house party."

"I saw on television," Tom said lifting his glass, "that most of 12th Street was burned to the ground -- like the neighborhood was bombed -- in a war."

"Yeah, it left a lot of people out on the street with nothing," Vern said, gulping his scotch, then wiping his chin, as he sat back in his chair heavily. "People in rich suburbs, I hear, are taking in black kids left homeless by the fires."

Tom looked away, and saw Bliss dancing with her father, and he remembered what Vern told him once, that her name came from Fort Bliss, Texas, where she was born while her father was stationed there in the Second World War. He was a lieutenant in the Military Police, he recalled, and that made him smile.

Wanting to say something positive, Tom, still smiling, said, "I went for a reporter job interview just after I got home from Spain -- at the <u>Detroit News</u>."

"How did it go?" Vern asked, as if interested, and Tom had to smile wider, thinking of Bliss' father, who was now the assistant Police Chief in a hick town near Ann Arbor, letting him marry his daughter.

"They said they'd call me," Tom said, trying not to grin. "The News wants to open a new Suburban Bureau -- and they need people who know the different areas. And I'm a shoo-in for the Grosse Pointes.

"I wrote for the weekly newspaper in Grosse Pointe -- when I was taking classes at Wayne State -- before I ran off to Spain."

"Uh-huh," Vern said sitting up straight, "but somehow -- you don't sound -- too enthusiastic, kiddo."

"Okay, you got me," Tom said. "I started a novel over in Spain -- I want to keep working on it. But I need time and a place to hide out while I write.

"I'm not enthusiastic about writing how the City Council votes on buying a new fire engine for the town."

Vern, grinning, looked attentive.

"You're still the suffering artist, huh?" he said.

"I guess so," Tom said reaching for his glass of scotch, "if you have to put a name on it."

"Hey, Tom -- why don't you come out to California? You know, take a look around -- if you dig it -- you might want to stay. At least it would get you away from newspaper writing here at home -- for awhile anyhow."

"That sounds cool," Tom said shaking his head slowly, "but I've got to get some money together. I'm flat broke."

"If you came out to Berkeley," Vern said getting excited by the idea, "you could live with us -- while you bum around, taking in the sights -- Jack London's haunts and all that.

"And who know, you might like the San Francisco scene -- and take roots."

"That's a neat offer," Tom said leaning on the table, "I could check out the hippies -- and the war protesters -- but first, I think I should see how things work out on this newspaper job. You know, -- if for nothing else -- to keep up appearances here at home."

Slightly dejected, Vern changed the subject, "What ever happened between you and that long-stem blond you were going with? That was a Grosse Pointe princess -- if I've ever seen one, kiddo."

"You got that right," Tom said and picked up his scotch glass, "I heard from somebody at Wayne State that she married some stockbroker -- and they live in New York City.

"I have a champagne taste -- but a beer budget -- when it come to women."

"She was a winner," Vern said, shaking her head.

"Before I went to Spain," Tom said looking over to where the dance floor had been cleared, and the bride and groom were alone, dancing in a spotlight, "we played tennis and were home, standing in the kitchen at her house, when her mother and sister came in -- after I had just told her my plans to visit Madrid."

"You were a dead duck, lad," Vern said slowly.

"Everybody in that kitchen -- including Skippy the dog -- knew I'd messed up."

Tom took a slow drink of scotch.

"In the weeks before I left," he said calmly, "she met this Superman from New York City -- somehow -- and <u>wham</u>, they were engaged.

"But she broke it off," Tom said leaning back in the chair, "and she and I went out -- in sort of a Bon Voyage move, and she told me the broker went nuts -- he even cried -- and offered her a wedding ring -- if she came back to him."

"You should have made your move," Vern said. "Make her your own."

"I had Spain on the brain," Tom said. "If I wrote a book that sells big -- my money and love problems would disappear -- that was my thinking at that time."

"Yeah," Vern said grinning, "a large lump of money works wonders."

"When my dad got sick with the kidney trouble," Tom said, "I waited a while, but he recovered, and I was packing for Spain again. Everyone was sure dad would not recover.

"I met Ann Calthrop at an art party -- where someone told me the booze was free in Birmingham, so I went there for just the drinking -- with Al Strassbaugh -- he paints and is always broke too."

"Ann and I hit it off from the start -- she's the only person I know who is wackier than I am; she never wears a bra."

Tom, grinning, looked up at the wedding decorations on the walls.

"She never wears a bra, huh?" Vern said smiling.

"That's what caught my eye," Tom said. "When I first met her --"

"Who never wears a bra?" Bliss asked. She had come over to the table without either of them seeing her. She had been sitting with her parents and the bride's mother and father.

"Just a girl I met at a party," Tom said making a sour face.

"I came to dance with my husband," Bliss said, "the floor is open again for everybody."

"I got to make a pit stop in the little boy's room," Vern said, getting up unsteady.

"You dance with me, Tom," Bliss said holding out her hand. "They're playing "Charmaine" -- that was one of my favorite songs in high school."

"I'm a little rusty at slow-dancing," he said getting up from the table, "but if you're that desperate, I guess I can't say no."

When they were moving with the other couples on the floor, Tom making sure he did not hold her too close, Bliss said to his face, "When am I going to dance at your wedding, you bum?"

"When I find a girl like you," he said.

"Oh-h, you can be sweet," she said pressing against him.

Feeling her soft breasts and down to her pelvis pressing, he started to feel excited. She was not slight, like most girls, her arms and legs round, that made her look sensuous. Combined with that she had a face with features that were sharp, that from any angle, was stunning.

Tom had to work hard to control himself.

Suddenly Bliss leaned back to look up at Tom's face, and said, "If you were married, you could move to California -- and buy the house next door to us in Berkeley."

"Yeah, it may be a while though," he said. "I think I just landed a job at the Detroit News -- they're supposed to call me -- any day now -- and let me know."

"Well," she said, "come out to San Francisco anyhow -- we'll show you around the sights."

Before Tom could speak, Vern tapped him on the shoulder.

"I'd like to dance with my wife," he said. When Bliss moved over to be held by Vern, he said smiling to Tom, "I'll never hear the end of it -- if I don't."

"Okay, lucky," Tom said smiling at Bliss, who was looking back over Vern's shoulder, smiling back.

CHAPTER 2

Two days after the wedding, Vern phoned Tom's house and his mother said he had been called to work at the <u>News</u>.

Vern told her he and his wife were leaving for the Canadian Exposition in Montreal, and would be back in three days.

The following day they came back to Detroit, Vern was unable to reach Tom at the newspaper, and because Bliss was anxious to see her children, they flew back to San Francisco.

At the newspaper, a woman phoned the Suburban Bureau, saying she was running for a seat on the Grosse Pointe Farms city council, and would like to talk to a reporter.

When Tom returned her phone call, she told him there was a serious blight problem in her city, and she would give him details, if he came to her house for an interview.

It was a Friday, when he walked up to the sprawling two-story house, wearing a sports coat and carrying a notebook, and rang the doorbell.

When the front door opened, he said, "Missus Mainwaring, I'm Tom Kemp from the <u>Detroit News</u>," then he saw her prosthetic arm, and a gray glove on a plastic hand.

He tried acting as if he had not noticed while walking across the parquet floor, keeping his eyes on her attractive face, until they entered the sun-filled sitting room.

He judged her age was no more than six years more than his own.

She sat down on the piano bench, across from Tom sitting on the couch, the sunshine flooding in behind her.

He noticed she sat at an angle that limited his view of the artificial arm to put him at ease.

"There is an abandoned shack," she said, "back at the edge of our property, where it meets the land owned by that stone church on the corner."

Nodding, Tom opened his notebook and began writing notes.

"That shack has been abandoned for years, and it's wood is rotting. I'm afraid now, that derelicts can hide in that shack -- or it could be used as a drug house.

"I'm concerned for the young children in the neighborhood, and I am campaigning to have it torn down."

When Tom finished writing, he said, "And that is your campaign promise -- to have the shack removed?"

"Yes," she said standing up from the bench, "you can see it from here. I'll show you."

He followed her to the bright windows, and with her good arm she pointed, "Any kind of people could use it -- even sleep -- in that hovel. You never know."

Tom squinted in the sunlight at the dark shack hidden by shadows of overgrown bushes and shaded by trees overhead.

It was the size of a garage with much of the wood covered with dark green moss, and on one corner the wood siding looked rotten.

The foreboding shack dated back to the turn of the century, when there had been small family plots of land in this neighborhood where the tenants grew vegetables to sell; that was why this section of Grosse Pointe was called "the farms" when it was incorporated into the city.

"It certainly doesn't belong there," Tom said.

"Yes," Missus Mainwaring said, "it's an eyesore in this community," as she smoothed the side of her hair with her good hand. "Particularly -- with the church being right there nearby."

"Right," Tom said, "I'll write the story for the newspaper -- maybe we can get the shack removed."

"It should have been removed long before now," she said as they walked toward the front door, Tom noticing her erect posture as he closed his notebook, wondering why she had lost an arm. It was disconcerting to wonder what happened to her.

He felt an overwhelming emotion to help her.

"I'll have a press photographer take a picture of the shack," he said, "to go along with the story I write. You may see a man moving around back there."

"I understand," she said while opening the front door.

"Bye," Tom said, and they shook hands, "and good luck in the election."

Sunday, the story and photo appeared in the Suburban Section of the newspaper, and when Tom looked close at the photo of the shack, it gave him a jolt.

The <u>News</u> photographer had taken the picture in the morning, and a mist off Lake St. Clair, two blocks beyond the stone church, made the shack look sinister, like a witches' house in the Black Forest.

Shaking his head, Tom said grinning, "It looks like a bunch of dwarfs will come out the door any second."

Monday morning, when Tom walked up to his desk at the newspaper office, he saw a note in his typewriter roller.

> All Further Stories Re The
> Grosse Pointes Must Be Approved
> By Boyce Covington's Desk
> Before Publication.
> B. Covington
> Managing Editor

Tom's boss, Houghton, the Suburban Editor, walked up when he saw him reading, "Geese, Kemp, I hear the phone was ringing at Covington's house all day Sunday. Covington's Grosse Pointe neighbors went crazy when they read that shack story -- and they wanted it removed at once."

Tom looked up from the note, saying, "All my stories have to be cleared by his desk?"

"He <u>owns</u> the paper, kid, that happens to be the twelfth largest in the country and he lives in Grosse Pointe. He can do anything he wants around here," Houghton said and shrugged.

"Man," Tom said, "I've only been here a couple of weeks, and I'm in hot water already."

"That's about the size of it Kemp," the editor said, turning and walking away.

Making the rounds of the city halls that week after the story appeared, Tom saw that the house was gone from the dark spot in the bushes.

At the end of the summer, when the elections were held, the lady with the artificial arm took eighty-seven percent of the votes, a landslide, winning a seat on the city council in the Farms.

A week later, a disgruntled employee in another suburb told Tom about a police car being crashed just after being repaired in a bump shop for a previous collision, and he began checking the story.

The informant was a shadowy wrecker-truck owner, named Keeler, who was running for a council seat himself, in the suburb west of the Grosse Pointes, but still on Tom's coverage area.

Asking questions, Tom found out the township cop crashed an unmarked police car on the way home from a party. Using township cars off-duty is prohibited, but the cop was the Police Chief's brother.

After the car was towed to a dealership to be repaired, the same cop was sent to pick it up, but the passenger door had a paint dead spot. The cop had to wait until a paint shop worker buffed the spot to a gloss, Tom found out.

The brother, and the cop who drove him to the dealership, slipped into a nearby bar while waiting.

During the two-hour wait, both cops drank too much, and by the time they went for the car, they were quite drunk.

After the Chief's brother signed for the car, Tom found out, he drove into the alley, speeding, and at the corner behind the dealership, crashed into a tow truck bringing another car to be repaired.

When Tom checked at the dealership, he found the township was billed over eight thousand dollars for the repairs for the two crashes of the police car; Keeler's tip was true.

Keeler then called Tom with more tips about mismanaged money in his township hall. Keeler had friends who worked for the township, who were passing him information with details of corruption going on.

Tom wrote news stores about the fraudulent goings-on, but when he turned them in to the Suburban Editor's desk, Houghton asked, "What does this Keeler guy want?"

"To be mayor, I guess," Tom said, as Houghton continued reading the typed pages.

"That's obvious," Houghton said, piling the pages together, then tapping the edges on his desk to make them even, "but we're not going to help him."

Houghton handed back the typed pages to Tom.

Two days later, Tom stopped by at Keeler's tow truck office to tell him what his editor said.

But what Tom did not know, was that another reporter, who worked for the Detroit news magazine FIRST ALERT, had been interviewing Keeler about the same township corruption stories, and had stepped into a side room when Tom knocked at the door.

"My paper won't print the stories you told me about the township corruption," Tom said to Keeler at his desk.

"How come?" Keeler asked, knowing the other reporter was listening.

"I'm not sure," Tom said shrugging, "but these guys should be exposed -- especially now -- before the election."

"All right," Keeler said, standing up behind his desk, then holding out his hand to shake Tom's. "I'll just have to try some other newspaper."

FIRST ALERT magazine was born when a newspaper strike left Detroit without any newspaper. The strike by editorial staff and reporters lasted over two years at the News.

The day-to-day events in Detroit were compiled in the weekly magazine's format and sold at newsstands.

Even though the <u>News</u> was back to publishing again for over a month, FIRST ALERT continued selling steady on the street, so the editors of the magazine kept printing it.

In the next week's copy of the magazine, after Tom had told Keeler of the refusal, a story appeared about the township corruption, and the reporter had included Tom's comment, "These guys should be exposed," along with the statement the <u>News</u> would not print it.

That afternoon, Houghton, the Suburban Editor, called Tom to his office.

"When we hired you on staff," Houghton said from behind his desk, "you recall you were told that your employment was only for a five-month trial period -- because we were unsure if a suburban news department would boost circulation.

"Well, it has been decided the suburban edition is not working out the way the paper wanted.

"So," Houghton said folding his arms, "five month's from your hiring date, your employment will be terminated."

"I'm being fired?" Tom asked, squinting in disbelief.

"The entire Suburban Bureau," Houghton said leaning back in his desk chair "is being eliminated -- by the Managing Editor."

"Damn," Tom said, feeling a cold shiver go down his spine.

He stood with his mouth open for a moment, thinking of what Houghton just said and how it would affect his life.

"By the way, Kemp," Houghton said, unfolding his arms, "I'd like to have that copy of what you wrote on that Keeler thing. We'll do a re-write -- print it, before the election over in that township."

Tom nodded.

Walking back to his desk, he tried to brush away the shock of losing his job, even though it was three months away.

He stood for a moment, looking around the newsroom, at the people typing at their desks, some talking on the phone, and realized all this would be lost.

"Shit," he said sitting down at his desk, "I don't feel like working. I don't give a damn anymore -- about this place."

He took the notes for the Keeler corruption story out of his desk drawer, and lifting his sports jacket off the back of the desk chair, walked across the press room, dropping the notes on the editor's desk as he headed for the door.

Driving out of the city, to where Jefferson Avenue turned into Lakeshore Drive, where the large estate houses began, he felt his newspaper work enthusiasm draining away.

Ahead, in the distance up the shoreline of Lake St. Clair, he looked at the spike tower of the Grosse Pointe Yacht Club, that was patterned after a structure of St. Mark's plaza in Venice, Italy, and said, "I don't belong here."

Driving slow in the right lane, he said, "How can a guy get psyched-up to dig for information to write, after he's told he's going to be out of work?"

Instead of making his rounds, stopping at city halls and police stations, he continued driving, passing through St. Clair Shores, out to where there were marinas, stocked with sail and power boats with For Sale signs.

When he saw the YARDARM nightclub over on the water's edge, he turned into the wide parking lot.

"I need a drink," he said. Then smiling, added, "I can put it on my expense account."

During the day, the YARDARM bar was open, but not the dance floor. And there was no band playing -- that hiked the prices.

While he was parking, he saw the dark squall clouds moving overhead, and before he climbed out of the car, a light drizzle of rain was falling on the windshield. He looked for a place to park near the bar entrance, but a Budweiser truck blocked the doorway, so he stopped where he was, climbed out, and ran for the door, his head down.

Inside the bar was dark, the only light from the big windows off to the right, across the dance floor, that overlooked the lake. He sat down on the nearest barstool.

He could see the rain coming, looking like a gray cloud, moving toward the shore.

"What'll you have?" the bartender in a white shirt asked.

"Rum and Coke."

"Twist of lime?"

Tom nodded, then looking down the bar, saw four men, all wearing suits, and he had to grin; they were all goofing off from work, like him.

Looking toward the windows across the dance floor, on the right, there were three tables with couples, silhouetted against the gray light of the lake.

Tom smiled remembering he and the Grosse Pointe girl came here. This place was far from Detroit. Nobody would recognize her, and because she was only twenty, and they did not check your identification for age.

The bartender put a wallop of Bacardi in the rum and Coke, but it did not help Tom get over the feeling he was given the bums-rush at the News, despite the fact the whole Suburban Bureau staff would be gone after three months.

He knew the previous two-year strike by editorial personnel was over wages. The reporters and editors tried to hold out, but after the first year, some realized they would never again get back the money they lost by striking, and they gave in.

Some editors and reporters took other newspaper jobs immediately after the strike began; they were the smart ones. The personnel, who waited for the strike to end, lost heavily during the strike that lasted two years.

"I'm not going to wait," Tom said picking his change up off the bar, feeling indignant. "Where's the telephone?" he asked the bartender, sliding off his barstool, shaking the coins in his hand.

"Out there in the lobby," the bartender said, pointing.

When Houghton came on the line, Tom said, "I can't work knowing my job is gone in a few months -- I can't work with that over my head.

"So, tomorrow, I won't report for work. I'm no longer working for the News."

Before the Suburban Editor could speak, Tom hung up.

*　　*　　*　　*　　*

At home, Tom's mother was upset over his losing the job, but after three days of his constant typing at a desk in the basement, she shouted down the stairwell.

"The neighbors think I'm hiding a fugitive in my basement. If your father was alive -- you wouldn't be hiding down there -- you'd be out looking for work.

"Your sister found a job a week after graduating high school -- and has been working ever since. Why can't you be like that?"

"I'm working on my book, mom," he said trying not to antagonize her.

"But you should have <u>some</u> kind of work, Thomas. Writing a book is not a job. A job pays money. And what do you think, when people hear that typing all day, they have to say about you?"

"Okay, Okay," he said nodding, "I'll make the rounds of some newspapers -- tomorrow -- look for a job.

"I'll even go to the Journalism Department over at Wayne State -- they get calls from publications who need writers all the time."

There was a silence.

"Can you drive me to the supermarket, Tom? I want to buy can goods that are on sale -- I need help carrying them."

"Sure, mom," Tom said leaning back in his chair. "Get the keys for dad's car."

He had returned the <u>Detroit News</u> car back to the garage, the morning after his phone call to Houghton, the Suburban Editor.

That evening, after dinner, Tom wrote a letter to Vern in San Francisco on the typewriter.

If your offer still stands for an all-expense tour of the Bay area, quickly send airline ticket.

Desperate.

CHAPTER 3

Tom looked up at the green and white sign overhead that read: OAKLAND, as he rode with Vern in the Porsche on the long metal bridge.

"And the lady across from me asked the stewardess if she could sit up in one of the roomy first class seats," Tom shouted to Vern. The Porsche was a convertible with the top down. "She said her legs were cramped -- so were mine, there's not much room in tourist class.

"There was hardly anyone up there -- I could see from where I was sitting," Tom said, watching Vern grin.

"What'd the stewardess say?" Vern shouted over the <u>whirring</u> of the tires on the grid metal of the bridge.

"She just nodded," Tom said, as Vern downshifted when they drove up behind a slow pick-up truck ahead. "And when the woman stood up, her husband helping her walk up the aisle way, I moved up behind them, and dropped into the first seat inside the First Class section doorway."

Vern accelerated the Porsche, shifting through the gears, "And the stewardess let you stay there?"

"She'd seen me stretching my legs out in the aisle," Tom shouted. "She knew I was uncomfortable in Economy Class -- or whatever the airline calls it."

"Hey, you got a break," he shouted.

"The best part," Tom shouted louder because the traffic had thinned out, and Vern was speeding, passing the other cars that appeared ahead, like they were standing still, "was dinner time.

"The Economy Class got ham sandwiches and a Coke, and us up forward had roasted chicken with asparagus, and a salad -- and best of all -- white wine in a plastic glass."

They were both smiling when Vern drove down the ramp to get off the bridge.

"You live around here?" Tom asked looking at the lights of the houses that shone from the dark hills.

"No," Vern said, "we live in the hills behind Berkeley -- Wildcat Canyon.

"The city water reservoir is back there too -- it looks like a lake off to the north of us."

Now that Tom was going to be a house guest, he had a sense of feeling that he should act appreciative; so he toned down how he spoke to Vern.

"I missed saying good-bye to you and Bliss," he said. "You left Detroit in a hurry."

"Yeah," Vern said quietly, "Bliss missed the baby, and our daughter Shelly -- we even cut short our tour of the Expo in Montreal by two days."

"You can't blame her," Tom said.

"I guess she felt guilty," Vern said, driving slower now in the dark streets, "about leaving the kids with a neighbor lady, who has a daughter the same age as our Shelly."

To change the subject, Tom said, "I brought the manuscript of my one-third finished novel -- it's in my suitcase.

"I brought it along," he said, "so I can work on it out here."

"Things must have been bad in Detroit -- at home?"

"The worst of it is I can't get any writing done back there without causing a ruckus," Tom said.

"Well, maybe your luck will change out here in sunny California -- that's what you're out here for, kid."

Tom nodded.

"Before we left Detroit," Vern said, "Bliss and I took a quick ride over to Twelfth Street -- to see how bad the riot damage was."

Tom winced, and was silent. Detroiters did not go to look at the tragic riot scene. It would be the equivalent of putting your hand in a wound.

Most Detroiters had seen enough on television, the burning, people looting stores and pushing shopping carts stacked with goods, the police standing, watching, shotguns at the ready, helpless, because of orders not to shoot.

Everybody in Detroit knew about the arrival of Federal troops, which meant a curfew enforced with an iron fist, and that it was the non-rioters who suffered.

When sniper shots allegedly were fired from a motel on Woodward Avenue near Boston Avenue, the paratroopers fired back with machine guns mounted on Jeeps.

People riding busses on Woodward Avenue after the motel shooting, looked up to the second floor window at the pock-marks where five people had died, until a week later, when the city tore the building down.

Most Detroiters avoided the part of the city where the riot happened, the neighborhood where storeowners suffered total losses at their businesses.

"Just after I graduated from Michigan," Vern said, as he brought the Porsche to an abrupt stop at a traffic light, jerking Tom forward, "I had a job -- insurance adjusting -- and I lived in an apartment near Twelfth Street. Before I had to go in the army."

"Yeah," Tom said grinning, "I remember. The company car was that light blue Plymouth -- that looked like a city police car."

They both laughed, as Vern sped away from the traffic light, going through the gears quickly.

"My old apartment house on Twelfth looked like it was hit by a bomb," Vern said, "the insides all burned black, and only part of one wall standing. Some riot, man."

"Well," Tom said to change the subject, "here you are out in golden -- California."

"Yeah, thanks to the army," Vern said turning off the street with heavy traffic, onto a road that seemed to skirt the bottom of the hills. "When I was drafted, they sent me out here to Fort Ord -- and put me in finance -- the payroll section.

"Bliss was still at home in Detroit -- but she flew out here to see me a couple of times -- until my army service was over."

"That's when you went to law school at Berkeley," Tom said. "Bliss told me."

"That's when Bliss and I got married," Vern said, "and she moved out here, while I was in law school."

"I remember that summer," Tom said. "I had a drink with her. I was on leave from the army -- just before I shipped to Germany."

Tom could see Vern did not like any references he made about Bliss, about seeing her alone.

"Well," Tom said, "at least you were lucky enough to <u>walk</u> out of the army -- they carried me out on a stretcher with that damn disease."

"Bliss was really shook up, kiddo," Vern said slowly, "after we visited you in the army hospital out there in Pennsylvania -- Valley Forge."

"Well," Tom said as they rode in the darkness now, no street lights, in hills where the houses were more scattered, "President Eisenhower said in a speech -- that it was better to carry a ninety-pound pack for two years in the army, than wear chains -- be a prisoner of some dictator."

"So we all have to serve -- two years."

When Vern turned onto the driveway that ran up to a lighted, spacious, ranch house above, Tom said quietly, "This is plush, man. You hit the jackpot -- right out of Law School."

"Well," Vern said, "I don't have a swimming pool -- yet."

He stopped in front of a closed garage door on the level below the house, and turned off the rear engined car.

"Bliss is waiting up for us," he said opening the car door on his side of the car. He paused, and then said, "I'll fill you in on my law bonanza -- later."

"Aren't you going to put the car in the garage?" Tom asked. "You don't leave this gem outside?"

"No room," Vern said getting out of the car, "the Mercedes is in there -- it's a big car -- four-door."

Tom blinked twice, and when he saw Vern pull the cloth top up on the Porsche, then reach up near the windshield to close the clamp, he did the same on his side of the car.

"You got a Mercedes too?" Tom said, shocked by Vern's wealth.

"Yeah," Vern said locking the Porsche door, "and there's a motorcycle in there too. I just thought of it. It's been neglected -- but you can use it to buzz around Berkeley."

"It may need a battery -- I'll check it."

Tom, looking up the steep steps to the house, said, "You got a Mercedes, a Porsche, and a friggin' motorcycle -- and look at this house. Man, you struck gold out here in California -- how much a year you make?"

"I don't know for sure, but my accountant does," Vern said leading the way up the steps. "I'm too busy to check."

At the top of the steps, they crossed a wide patio that had the pattern of the sun at the center, with different colored stones radiating out making up the floor. In the light from the house, Tom saw shrubs enclosing the patio and tall trees behind the shrubs.

"Impressive," Tom said. "You live like a movie star."

Vern pushed   open the heavy wood door shouting, "Bliss -- we got company."

"I'm in here," she said.

Tom followed Vern across the foyer, looking up at the chandelier, then down at the maroon carpeting.

Bliss was sitting on a couch in the sunroom that had a glass door at the far end that opened out on a back patio.

She was holding the baby, Frederick, while closing her quilted robe with her free hand.

"Well," she said getting up, "you finally came out to see us -- you'll like it out here in California."

She kissed Tom on the lips, as Vern was taking the baby from her arm; the same kind of short kiss she gave him at the Valley Forge army hospital.

He remembered pulling down the facemask he had to wear, before she kissed him, standing there in the hospital bathrobe in the hallway when they came to visit.

"You're looking super," Tom said, "as usual," watching her back away from him, noticing the compliment did not faze her.

She had a look of consternation; a fold between her eyes, her jaw set, when she said to Vern, "there was someone watching me from the patio -- while I was breast-feeing the baby tonight."

Tom could see she was angry and afraid as she took the child Frederick from Vern, slowly.

"What am I going to do?" she said to Vern's face. "What if someone tries to get in the house when you're not here?"

"I'll take a look around outside," he said walking over to the heavy glass patio door, unlocking it, sliding it open, stepping out into the dark outside.

"I'm glad <u>you're</u> here Tom," Bliss said putting her hand on his arm. "Vern is gone a lot -- you'll be the protection for the house."

"Maybe it was just somebody," Tom said, "out looking for a lost dog or cat."

Then he realized what he had said; he admitted <u>someone</u> had been outside the patio door.

She looked at him for an instant, but did not speak, while lifting the baby higher, using both her arms now.

Vern came in, scraping his feet at the patio door after walking in the dirt beyond the edge of the back patio.

"There were no cars, I could see in either direction on the road, from the edge of the hill," he said. After pulling the glass door closed, he locked it, and drew the drapes closed.

"Keep the drapes closed at night," he said walking over to Bliss. Then putting a hand on her shoulder, he said quietly, "I'll call the police -- make a report of a prowler -- ask them to patrol the neighborhood for a few nights."

"That would help," she said, "knowing the police are around."

"I'll call right now," he said going to a doorway at the end of the sitting room near the front door. "I'll be with you in a minute, Tom. We'll have a drink."

When Tom heard him dialing the phone, the study light on, he could see books on shelves, lining a wall behind a desk.

"I think I saw someone once before," Bliss whispered to Tom, "but I wasn't sure. But this time -- I am."

"You should buy a gun," Tom said, his head to one side.

She nodded, as if thinking about a gun, then said, "I'm going to put the baby to bed."

"Sorry about all this hullabaloo, Tom -- on the night of you coming to California. There's whiskey in that cabinet behind the couch. Help yourself."

"Don't talk like that," he said watching her walk across the room to a hallway.

Tom was pouring scotch into a glass, when Vern came out into the sitting room, walking up behind him, "The police said a car will come here tomorrow morning -- to make a report."

"Where's Bliss?" he asked taking a glass to pour himself a drink.

"Putting the baby to bed," Tom said handing him the bottle.

"I told the cops I looked around the patio, but it's dark -- I couldn't see footprints -- something like that."

Tom watched him almost fill his glass with scotch, before he set it back in the cabinet.

They were both sipping scotch, when Vern said, "Heck of a first night in San Francisco, kid, but don't let this prowler thing dampen your visit out here."

To ease Vern's embarrassment, Tom said, "Maybe it's just some disgruntled client of yours --"

"Could be," Vern said pointing to the couch, "I never thought of that."

They both were sitting down at opposite ends of the couch, "You never know who has an axe to grind -- in this legal business," Vern said gravely. "You can't satisfy everybody."

"What makes it worse though, is that I'm away from home so much. Bliss keeps carping at me about being gone -- but it's part of what I have to do in my business."

"Man," Tom said, "you've really done tremendous in a short time -- you just have to look around to see that -- this house -- the cars -- your family. The absences -- that's the price for -- success."

"I fell into it," he said. "Success came to me, you could say."

"I don't follow," Tom said, looking at the amount of scotch he had left in the glass.

"After law school here at Berkeley -- after I graduated -- it took me two times before I passed the State Bar Exam -- and the first job I got was with the Lumberman's Union. I was the assistant to the lawyer, and things went smooth most of the time -- I was home at night mostly, until contract negotiation time. Then it turned into hours at the bargaining table, me doing research for my boss, with -- sometimes a trip to Washington D.C. to confer with the Labor Relations Board."

"So Bliss got ticked-off about you being away so much," Tom said lifting his foot, resting it on his other leg at the knee. "That's kind of understandable -- you can't blame her."

"Yeah," Vern said, taking hold of his glass with both hands, "she had to run everything here at home by herself. But there was one thing -- I kept telling her -- that it was just for a short time -- we were negotiating a new contract."

"So she backed-off, huh?"

"Yeah, and I was making such good money -- it would be stupid to quit -- I told her. In fact, I was way ahead, in the money department, of most of the other guys in my law class. The faculty, who taught my class, even asked me to speak a couple times on labor law negotiations to the students."

"So at work," Tom said feeling the effect of the scotch, "you were king -- and at home you were -- a stranger."

"Then things -- got more complicated," Vern said.

"What do you mean?"

"My boss had a damn heart attack," Vern said shaking his head. "And three weeks later -- he died."

"Don't tell me -- kid."

"You guessed it," Vern said grinning, "the union figured I knew most of the problems the union faced, and that I should take over the reins; do my dead bosses' job."

"So that's what you meant -- when you said success fell into your hands? How lucky can you get?"

"Yeah, but it hit our house like a bomb," Vern said and took a long drink of scotch.

"Bliss was glad about the promotion part, but I knew she was thinking about the long absences that came with it. I could tell, even thought she tried not to show it -- I could read it in her reactions as time went by -- it was eating her up."

"There was nothing you could do," Tom said finishing the scotch in his glass.

"I couldn't quit," Vern said, shrugging, "that would be stupid. I told myself I'd make it up to her -- but -- the absences got longer --"

"And now you're worried -- you might lose her, huh?"

"That's about it in a nutshell, man."

CHAPTER 4

Bliss came into the sitting room and walked over to the couch where Tom and Vern sat.

Tom noticed she washed her face, and combed her hair back. She was wearing a sheer yellow gown that had layers so that her shape was completely hidden.

Her face was soft again.

"You guys better lay-off the drinking," she said while standing in front of them. "The weekend is just beginning -- you two will be like wilted lettuce by Sunday."

"You're right, babe," Vern said while half-moving forward off the couch, holding his scotch glass low. "I thought we all -- the kids too -- would enjoy a ride down to Monterey, do a little sight-seeing. Carmel too."

The phone rang over in Vern's study.

"Now what?" he said getting up, setting his drink on a side table. "I'll be back in a flash," he said walking away to his office.

Bliss looking down at Tom, said, "Come out to the kitchen -- I'll scramble some eggs -- and make coffee."

"You don't have to fuss," Tom said leaning forward on the couch, "that prowler thing put everybody on edge."

"I can't let a window-peeper upset me," she said, "keep me from entertaining a friend who has just travelled here for a visit -- now can I. You must be starved."

Turning, she said, "Come out to the kitchen -- you can bring your drink."

Getting up to follow her, Tom said, "I had some wonderful rubber chicken on the plane," while watching how her gown billowed as she walked to the kitchen door, then snapping on the light.

"In that gown," Tom said, "you look like you're in a movie scene."

Grinning, he sat down at the table, still holding his scotch glass.

"I thought I'd give that gawker on the patio something to gawk at," she said smiling, bending to take a skillet out of a low cabinet.

When Tom saw she was not wearing anything under the gown, as it pulled tight on her bottom, the sudden feeling the <u>he</u> was the intruder -- the one imposing on a family's intimate life. Something told him he better be careful.

Vern walked into the kitchen, "that was Charlie Bellows; he was in my law class at Berkeley," he said looking at Bliss.

"He phoned at this hour to ask what I think about him taking a job in Washington D.C.," Vern sipping from his scotch glass.

"When he graduated -- scrounging for a law job -- he applied to Washington -- and now they answered him -- and he said they want his answer by Monday. The letter just came today," Vern said calmly.

"And he doesn't know if he wants it or not -- right?" Bliss said, breaking eggs, over the hot butter sputtering in the frying pan, dropping them in. "And he wants you to decide."

"I guess so," Vern said, sipping from his scotch glass, sitting down at the table at the same time. Looking across at Tom, he said, "I guess you could say that," and shrugged.

"Vern," Bliss said stirring the eggs, "you should explain to him -- you're not the father-confessor for your whole law class from over there at Berkeley. Tell Charlie he has to make his own choices."

"You're not saying that," Vern said, making a grimace at Tom, "because you don't want him butting-in our time together while -- I'm home -- are you?"

Tom knew Vern had too much scotch now; he hoped Bliss realized it too.

Disregarding what Vern said, Bliss turned and commented, "You should tell Charlie you have an out-of-town guest," while she was stirring the thickening eggs.

"Yeah," Vern said capitulating, "you're right, babe. I should have thought of that."

Tom, watching Vern sipping from his scotch glass, was wishing he could be someplace else but here. Living off other people's largess had a price, he thought, and being in the middle here, was the cost.

"Make toast Vern, if you want some," Bliss said in a matter-of-fact manner, lifting the skillet off the flame.

"I can fry bacon, if you guys want," she said giving them the eggs piled in the pan, "I got the pre-fried kind -- it's frozen. I just have to warm it."

"Tom can't have meat on Friday," Vern said while turning to put four slices of wheat bread into the toaster. "He's a Catholic."

"He had chicken on the flight from Detroit," Bliss said, putting a scoop of eggs on Tom's plate, smiling down at him.

"I forgot," Tom said, looking at the steaming eggs on his plate. "Besides, I haven't been to church -- in a long time."

Seeing Tom uneasy talking about religion, Bliss changed the subject, saying, "What department is Charlie applying for in Washington?"

"I'm not sure," Vern said while piling his scrambled eggs on his toast to make a sandwich."

"The Bureau of Weights and Measures," Tom said.

They all laughed.

"That was cute, Tom," Bliss said from over at the sink, where she was running water into the frying pan.

"We're so glad you came out here. Oh -- yes we're glad. We need you to say things like that."

She seemed different somehow, out in California than she did in Detroit, Tom thought, smiling up at her. She was not her carefree demeanor out here; quite the opposite, she acted like she was carrying a heavy responsibility.

When Vern finished his egg sandwich, he stood up, and wiping his face said, "I'm going to call Charlie Bellows -- tell him we won't be home until real late Sunday. I told him to come by in the evening, but I'll cancel that."

When he was out of the kitchen, Tom said to Bliss, "Is Kyle Browning still out here in California?"

"Uh-huh," she said, and they both laughed.

She was sitting at the table, holding a cup of coffee, "And he's still selling those encyclopedias -- in fact he won the office contest for a week in Mexico -- a vacation for his whole family.

"And his wife, Doris, is expecting their second child -- but she's still working -- she teaches third grade in some school here in Marin County. I'm not sure where."

Kyle Browning was a Grosse Pointer who never had a steady job; that was why Tom and Bliss laughed. He worked when he needed money, but otherwise spent the day playing tennis, or betting at the horse race track.

When Kyle was drafted into the army, he worked as a helicopter mechanic stationed in California, and he sent for his wife, and after his army service and with their first child, they stayed and settled in Oakland.

He met Doris at Central Michigan college, but he was drafted when he dropped out, even though he was married.

Kyle had a 1941 Ford Coupe with a souped-up engine, and he met Tom and Vern at Cupid's drive-in on the east side of Detroit.

"It'll be fun talking to him," Tom said. "We used to burn up the streets -- drag racing."

Vern came in the kitchen doorway, saying quietly, "Charlie insists on coming over Sunday night -- no matter how late. He's got a client meeting all day Saturday in Sacramento, so he said Sunday is the only day we can talk, make a decision for Monday to Washington."

He sat down at the table, looking at Bliss.

"We should be home by eight - nine o'clock Sunday night from our trip."

Bliss stood up, and pushing her chair under the table, said, "I'm going to bed. I've got to get up with Shelly for her dance lesson tomorrow. She gets so excited the night before her class, she can hardly sleep."

"How old is she now?" Tom asked.

"Four."

"She's dancing kind of early," Tom said.

"This is California," Bliss said, before she walked out of the kitchen, "everybody has to start early."

Vern, leaning back in his chair, said "I usually go into my office for half a day on Saturday -- so you'll have to manage for yourself until noon. We'll all be back by then."

"Do what you have to do," Tom said waving his hand to act casual. "Don't worry about me, sluggo."

"C'mon, I'll show you the motorcycle," Vern said getting up from the table. "I haven't used it -- since I bought the Porsche. The battery might need charging."

When he snapped on the light in a narrow stairway, Tom followed him down the cement steps.

"It's a Bultaco," he said when they stepped onto the floor of the garage that smelled musty in the dampness, "made in Spain.

"Kyle bought one -- they cost only three hundred bucks -- so I picked up one too."

"Man," Tom said, "that's cheap -- for a motorcycle."

"Yeah, it's kind of a workingman's bike over there in Spain," Vern said, squeezing around the gunmetal gray Mercedes, that took up most of the garage space.

"All the screw tops fit a quarter. You can take the entire bike apart with a quarter -- you don't need tools."

When Tom slid out of the narrow space between the cement wall and the big car, he saw the dusty motorcycle.

Vern pumped the starter pedal, and the motor started, sputtering, filling the air with gray smoke.

"Hey, man, it runs," Vern shouted, then turned the key to shut it off. "You're in luck -- you just have to wipe off the dust."

"How lucky can you get," Tom said grinning.

Taking off the gas cap, Vern shook the machine, then put his finger in the tank, saying, "About a third full."

"Great," Tom said grinning. "Hey, this takes me back to the hot rod days in high school -- all the drag racing we did -- when we were kids at Denby."

Vern, swinging his leg to get off the motorcycle, "Yeah, that was a ball with that old thirty-four Ford."

"We were lucky -- to stay out of jail."

Tom remembered how Vern's father, the lawyer, let him use the garage to build a hot rod, parking his Chrysler in the driveway.

Tom had a paper route, and Vern worked part time trimming trees, and they scraped together fifty dollars to buy a 1934 Ford Sedan and took the old engine, a V-eight, and went hunting in junkyards for a bigger engine.

They found a smashed 1949 Mercury, took the engine out at the junk yard, and hauled it home. After having the block bored for bigger pistons, they put the bigger block into the 1934 Ford Sedan.

Vern bought a three-quarter-race camshaft with part of his college saving money; a full-race camshaft was illegal for street driving. On the dual-carburetor manifold, they installed two Holly carburetors. A neighbor, who worked at Holly, <u>gave</u> them to Vern, after one night coming into the garage to look over the car one evening.

Holly carbs were unique; they <u>sprayed</u> fuel into the engine manifold, not squirting gas into the engine like a regular carb.

A Blue-Streak coil, and four-pronged Bosch spark plugs, completed the engine soup-up, followed by a heavy-duty clutch, and the cutting down the stick-shift handle to eleven-inches for cramp shifting when drag racing.

The 1934 Ford had a standard four-eleven gear ratio in the rear differential; perfect for drag racing.

During the time they were building the car, teachers at Denby High School pulled a surprise locker inspection -- looking for drugs. When the locker Tom and Vern shared was opened, wrenches, copper tubing, an old fuel pump, and stacks of car instruction manuals were found, and they were sent to the Principal's Office to explain.

But the only thing that was illegal on the car they were building was the brakes. The 1934 Ford had standard mechanical brakes, and the law required hydraulic brakes.

But hydraulics were too expensive to install, so Tom and Vern decided to let the brake problem slide. Besides, they were eager to get on the road with the car, see what it would do.

Hot rod cars were cruising Woodward Avenue in the 1950 era, out in the suburbs of Oakland County, north of Detroit. Some of the vehicles were Custom Cars, with leaded-in hoods where emblems and chrome had been, for a sleek look; chopped tops to lower the car profile and windows, even spring shackles that made the car body just hover over the ground.

Most Custom Car owners bragged they had twenty-seven or more coats of lacquer paint on their cars for the luster that glistened.

The girls like to ride in the Custom Cars, as the owners drove around Drive-In restaurant parking lots to show off all along Woodward Avenue.

But these Custom Cars were not hot-rods -- race cars.

Whenever a hot-rod came to a stop at a traffic light, the driver would rev his engine, and if the drive next to him did the same, a race was on.

On the green light, the two cars, tires screeching, would race to the next light.

The police were always on the watch for illegal street racing from Royal Oak all the way out Woodward Avenue to the plush suburb of Birmingham to the north of Detroit.

Tom remembered one race with the 1934 Ford on an outlaw road called "Northwestern Highway" in a new subdivision being built just north of the Detroit city limits.

The "Highway" was nothing more than a stretch of paved road out in open country. There were no curbs on the side of this road, no streetlights, and no traffic. It was a desolate stretch of pavement to nowhere, running four miles.

Tom and Vern heard racing was going on at Northwestern -- for money -- so they drove out on a Friday night to the Sunrise Restaurant. The meeting point for drag racers.

In the parking lot of the cinder-block restaurant, all styles of racing cars were parked, some painted brightly, some with mat-grey primer, but most of the engines had chrome parts that glistened in the lights.

A thin man named Lempke, asked Vern what he was running in the grotesque old Ford, and after Vern told him, the thin guy held out fifty dollars -- betting he could beat Vern.

Tom remembered saying as they rolled out of the parking lot to the dark stretch of roadway, "This is going to be like taking candy from a baby.

"He's got a 1949 Ford with dual carbs -- and a leaded-in hood where he took off the emblems and primed it with gray paint."

They both laughed.

Tom was to cram-shift through the gears; Vern had to hold the steering wheel with both hands to keep the light-weight old Ford on a straight line.

Tom remembered looking out at the pitch-black stretch of road ahead in the headlights, at the same time watching Lempke's buddy in the other car holding a white handkerchief up, out of the window.

When the handkerchief dropped, the two cars jumped, side by side, tires screeching, then Vern shouted, "Shift," and Tom crammed the Ford into second gear, and the 1934 Ford lurched ahead of the other car.

When Vern yelled, "Shift," again, Tom could see the headlights of the 1949 Ford way behind.

"Candy from a baby," Vern shouted, taking his foot off the accelerator, letting the car slow.

"Fifty-bucks worth of candy," Tom remembered saying.

Now, in California, Vern was going up the cement steps of the garage to the house, when he said, "I leave about eight in the morning for the office -- and Bliss about a half-hour later for the dance class -- so you're on your own in the morning."

"I'll manage," Tom said.

"What happened to that leggy, Grosse Pointe girl you were going with?" Vern asked when they came to the top of the steps.

"She married some guy from New York City," Tom said closing the door. "She was in a hurry to marry -- and I went to Spain.

"She said the guy was a stockbroker, but I think he was a cop -- even worse -- a Fed, maybe."

"What do you mean, kid?"

"I don't know," Tom said. "All the time at Wayne University -- I had the feeling I was being watched. When she and I went out, there seemed to be some guy near, listening to what we were saying."

"What would the cops or Feds -- want with you?"

"Maybe it was something about that damn lung disease I caught in Germany -- maybe they think I'm a spy-disease spreader. Or maybe it was the army watching me. I don't know for sure."

"So you got this Ann for a girl now?"

"Yeah, she sent a postcard to my folks house in Detroit when I was in Spain, saying she was 'studying the Etruscans in Italy.'"

"She a college grad?"

"Yeah," Tom said as they walked across the sitting room, "she went to Brown. She wants to teach painting on the university level."

Vern picked up his near empty scotch glass off the table next to the couch, and drank what was left.

"If I would have know Ann was in Italy -- when I was down in Spain -- I would have travelled up to see her."

"You told her about your writing -- how you want to write novels, huh?"

"Yeah, and I lucked-out," Tom said folding his arms. "She knows all about my bumming around -- but she claims she's not planning to get married until she's twenty-four.

"Her plan is to get educated before she settles down with a family to raise."

Tom felt uncomfortable talking about Ann -- he felt as if he were being cross-examined in court.

"She sounds right for you, kid," Vern said setting down the scotch glass. "You both like the art scene. What's her name?"

"Ann Calthorp -- her family has roots in New England; Boston," Tom said softly.

CHAPTER 5

After Tom showered and pulled on a golf shirt the next morning, he walked out to the kitchen, seeing the wall clock at ten-seventeen.

He picked up an empty cereal box laying on the floor near the table, smiling, and found the other cereal box on the table was half full, corn flakes, and he went to the side cabinet, looking for a bowl.

When he saw the brown bottle of Christian Brothers brandy on the shelf, he poured the brandy into a bowl, then shook corn flakes on top of the liquor.

"'Breakfast of Champions?'" he said sipping the soggy corn flakes.

As he finished the last of the cereal, he saw over the edge of the bowl, that the bright sun was drying the wet patio dampness; someone had pulled back the curtain.

Unlocking the glass door, he pulled it back, "Ah, so this is sunny California," he said, stretching his arms. "The Golden State. Wow!"

In almost a week, it would be Halloween, and here it was almost like summer, not dreary like back home in Michigan, and he shook his head, smiling.

Slowly, he walked over to the edge of the patio to where Bliss said she saw the intruder last night.

He looked for a moment at the man-sized shrubs, then walked out past them, into a stand of Pine trees that had shed needles and cones to cover the ground, then over to the edge of a cliff that dropped eighty or ninety feet to a tar road below.

Off to his left, he saw a wide V-shaped ditch that must have been carved by run-off rainwater that ran down the cliff to the road.

He stood, thinking that whoever climbed up, must have used the ditch to get to the patio of the house.

He stood for a moment, looking at the bare dirt in the ditch and was about to turn away, when he saw a thin black tube laying at a sharp angle.

He bent down, and picking it up, found it was a ballpoint pen. It was not the kind used in an office, a long plastic tube, but the style carried in a shirt pocket.

The pen clip was rusty, and caked with mud underneath.

Using a thumb to clean away the mud, he saw white letters:

US GOVERNMENT

"Vern is being watched," Tom said. "This pen has been here a while -- long enough to rust."

He looked again down at the roadway, just as a pickup truck was passing, hauling an old refrigerator.

Turning to walk back to the house, he looked at the pen again.

"If the intruder is a Fed," Tom said, "why the hell is Vern being watched?"

Walking onto the patio, he said, "I wonder what the hell he's done now?"

Tom caught himself, and grinned, "Hey, I better stop playing the snooping reporter -- I'm a guest here."

Inside the house again, pulling the glass door closed, he had a sense of foreboding: it was not his being in California -- it was more universal than that -- his life style did not seem to fit <u>anywhere</u>.

His life was movement, never settling in one place too long, where the trouble of the place, he always found, would creep over you -- involve you.

"Well, I'm out here now," he said, going to the cabinet where the brandy bottle was, taking a sip.

"I can at least see the California sights -- and the Jack London places.

"That'll boost my morale -- seeing how London made it through life -- seeing how another writer made it; his way."

Putting the brandy bottle back on the shelf, Tom said, "I can't stay out here in San Francisco, live here, it isn't in the cards.

"But I owe Vern a fair trial -- for bringing me out for a look-see. Besides, it won't hurt to visit all the places around the Bay -- soak-up what life is like out here."

He laughed, saying, "It's almost like I'm <u>stealing</u> California."

Looking at the ballpoint pen he set on the sink when taking the brandy bottle, he picked it up.

"I wonder if this is a harbinger -- of some kind of trouble to come? I'll show it to Vern -- see what he thinks -- the reason for it being there. Geez, a government pen!"

He put the pen on the shelf next to the brandy bottle.

"Now, I'm going to just be a tourist," he said looking out the kitchen window at the sunshine. "Besides, it's not every day you can buzz around Berkeley on a motorcycle."

After pulling a dark-blue windbreaker from his suitcase in the bedroom, Tom walked down the steps to the inside of the garage.

Sunlight flooded the damp garage when he lifted open the wide door. He wheeled out the Bultaco, and while wiping off the dust, he saw a police car come up the drive slowly and stop.

"Are you here about the peeping-tom call last night?" he asked the short policeman, who came walking toward him, pulling up his heavy black belt that held his gun, handcuffs, and a can of Mace.

"Did you call in the complaint?" he asked, taking a notebook out of his shirt pocket.

"No, I'm Tom Kemp, a house guest here from Detroit. The homeowner, Vern Hurley, had just picked me up at the airport, when --"

"What time was that?"

"Just after nine o'clock -- it was dark -- and when we came into the house, Vern's wife, Bliss, said she saw someone out on the patio -- as she was feeding their youngest child."

The policeman who had driven the car, came up, and hearing what Tom said, asked, "Can you show us the patio?"

"Alright," Tom said dropping the wiping rag on the motorcycle seat. "This way," he said before leading them back to the garage cement steps.

Upstairs in the sitting room, Tom pointed to the couch, saying, "Bliss was sitting there feeding the baby," and as he crossed the room to the glass door, he added, "this curtain was back like this --"

"Was the door locked?" the short policeman asked.

"Yes," Tom said, even though he was unsure. "And Bliss said the curtain was open, left open from the daytime to let in sunlight."

"Where was the intruder standing?" the driver policeman asked, looking through the glass door.

Tom pulled open the door, leading them out on the patio.

"Here," Tom said. "Bliss said she saw the outline of a man -- standing here by this tall shrub -- looking."

"Were there footprints?" the short cop asked.

"No," Tom said. "The husband, Vern, after we came from the airport, and the wife told him about the peeping-tom -- went out to check the patio bushes. When he came back inside, he said there were no footprints he could see."

"He wouldn't be able to see prints in the dark," the driver cop said.

"There are bright overhead lights all around the patio," Tom said. "He had turned them on."

"Okay," the short policeman said, putting his notebook back in his shirt pocket. "We'll write the report -- and the detective bureau might send a man by later."

"The family will all be here at home for lunch," Tom said leading the policeman to the front door.

He pulled open the door, looking at the police car for a moment, down in the driveway.

"If you have any more questions about --"

"The detective might have some background information questions," the short policeman said going out the door.

"Tell the family we'll increase our night patrols in this neighborhood," the driver cop said before stepping out the doorway.

"Okay," Tom said, "I'll tell them."

He watched the police car from the door, as it turned around and drove down to the end of the sloping driveway.

"They're probably wondering," he said smiling, "what the hell I'm doing here."

He closed the door.

Driving the motorcycle, Tom had trouble shifting the gears, as he started rolling down the driveway from the house. He could not find the correct position with his toe on the kick-shift gearbox, and hit the lowest gear. He lunged forward over the handlebars, almost falling, after he shifted in first gear mistakenly.

"Dammit!" he shouted, stopping the Bultaco at the road where the house driveway ended.

"It's been a while since I've driven a toe-shift bike," he said to himself, slowly pressing the lever with his toe, to get the feel of the three gear positions while holding the clutch in neutral.

When Tom looked up the road for oncoming cars, he saw a silver Monte Carlo pull off and stop, up where the wash near Vern's patio came down hill.

He watched as the men stepped out of the Monte Carlo, seeing both had brush haircuts, one wearing a gray suit, the other in a brown sports jacket. They walked, looking at the wash.

"Cops," he said. "Probably detectives."

Slowly, he drove the motorcycle in the opposite direction from them, gradually increasing speed, going through the gears.

He stopped, then started again, moving through the three gears rapidly to gain top speed on the bike.

"I think I got the gears now," he said while coming to a stop, looking around at the hills. "Maybe I won't go too far -- I might get lost out here in the sticks. I don't see any road signs."

Vern's Porsche came around the turn up ahead, and stopped suddenly next to the motorcycle.

"Got the hang of the kick-shift?" Vern asked grinning. "They're a little tricky."

He had the convertible top down again, and was wearing the kind of sunglasses that change to dark in the light, by a chemical in the laminated lenses.

"Okay, okay," Tom said. "It took a few tries -- but I got the positions."

"Want to race?"

"Better watch it, man," Tom said evenly, "I think I saw a couple of detectives near the house, looking around."

Vern's grin faded.

"Right," he said, "I better run. Talk to them."

He sped away.

The Porsche was parked beside the house front steps, when Tom rode the cycle up the hill. He saw Vern talking with the detectives, standing at the side of the house, as he slid off the Bultaco, and figured they must have climbed the hill while looking around.

Walking up, he heard the detective in the suit, saying, "Have you had any trouble with the neighbors?"

"I'm not home much," Vern said. "I really haven't had much contact with the neighbors."

The detective in the suit looked at Tom

"He's a house-guest," Vern said. "When we came last night from the airport, my wife told me about -- the intruder."

The detective in the sports jacket had looked at Tom for a moment; he was writing in a notebook.

He asked Vern, "Are you aware of any disgruntled clients -- your legal work?"

"No, no," Vern said. "I'm a labor lawyer. I do contract negotiations for the lumber worker's union -- I don't have any contact with the rank and file."

"I see," the detective in the suit said, looking at Vern's sunglasses turning darker with the sun getting higher over the house.

Then the detective with the notebook, while closing it, putting it in his jacket pocket, squinted at Vern saying, "Has your wife even had any trouble with an old boy friend? Some -- unwanted suitor?"

"No," Vern said shaking his head. "She's never mentioned anything like that to me."

The detective in the suit took a card out of his top pocket and, handing it to Vern, said, "If you think of anyone who might have been out on the patio, call us at this phone number."

Watching the two detectives walking down the driveway incline, looking off at the dark shrubs on both sides as if expecting to spot a thug lurking there, Vern held up the card, saying to Tom, "Okay, Detective Sergeant Brian Ellis," while reading it.

"He's just doing his job," Tom said grinning.

"Maybe it's their attitude," Vern said. "I still have trouble talking to cops."

"They sure gave us a bad time with the old thirty-four Ford."

"You can say that again," Vern said shaking his head. "Hey, Bliss phoned me at the office -- she wants to take the kids clothing shopping this afternoon -- so I said I'd show you around some of Berkeley.

"Tomorrow, all of us will ride down to Monterey, okay?"

"Great," Tom said. "Monterey is Steinbeck country -- the place he wrote about in his fiction stores -- where he loved and learned."

Vern pointed toward the house, "Let's have a cold one before we buzz around Berkeley," and started for the steps up to the house.

"I forgot to tell you," Tom said, following Vern, "this morning when I looked around the patio, I found something back in the woods."

"What did you find?" Vern said when opening the front door.

"I put it next to the brandy in the kitchen."

In the kitchen, Tom took the pen and handed it to Vern.

"It's just a pen, Tom."

"Read the side. I found it in the mud by that rain run-off culvert."

"'US Government'" Vern said. "So what? It could have been dropped anytime -- there are surveyors down on the road all the time. They set up a transit and shoot the level of the water over in the reservoir -- checking on how much the water dropped."

"But I didn't find it on the road," Tom said defiantly. "I found it up at the <u>top</u> of the hill -- in the wash."

"Aw-w, they check that too," Vern said, setting the pen on top of the refrigerator, then pulling open the door.

"Here, kid, have a Budweiser -- and quit trying to make a mystery story out of a ballpoint pen.

"There are State and Federal guys climbing all over these hills -- they're on watch for forest fires. They check the woods and trees' dryness -- stuff like that."

"Okay," Tom said nodding, "I didn't know."

He popped open the beer can.

"Relax, man," Vern said after taking a long drink of beer, then setting the can on the sink. "Quite acting like a news reporter -- enjoy it out here.

"We'll go for a buzz -- after I change this shirt," he said pulling off his tie. "I'll show you Berkeley."

When Vern went to the bedroom, Tom picked up the pen from the top of the refrigerator to look at it.

"Wish I could be as sure -- as you are, kid," then he took a sip of beer.

"Something ain't right around here," Tom said looking at the pen. "Something's going on."

CHAPTER 6

Sunday morning, Tom went with Vern and his family to a downtown Berkeley waffle shop, where Vern said it was a tradition for the teaching faculty families to come for breakfast. The restaurant was crammed with people.

From the table, Tom watched as the kids at the other tables poured all the different flavors of syrup from the racks on the same waffle on their plates, while their fathers, like Vern, sat engrossed in the thick edition of the New York Times.

Bliss sat across from Tom, the baby Frederick next to her in a high chair, and when the waffles arrived, began cutting his waffle into pieces, while she was talking to a woman in a tan suit bending over her shoulder.

Tom winced, listening to the din of talking filling the room, punctuated by an occasional shout by one of the children, and the clatter of dishes being dumped from trays out in the kitchen.

Tom noticed other people began table-hopping after eating breakfast, talking to other parents, bending over their shoulder to speak, like the lady in the tan suit. It seemed to be part of the tradition, Tom thought.

"A hell of a way to spend Sunday morning," he muttered to himself, cutting a piece of waffle with his fork.

Yesterday was not too beneficial either; Tom failed to act impressed on the trip around Berkeley with Vern in the Porsche.

Vern had stopped at the university gate, so Tom could look up to the Greco-Roman building dominating the Berkeley campus, the site of the protests against the Vietnam War, and Tom had blurted, "It looks almost like the same building the Columbia campus has."

To Tom, the pillars and façade looked a duplicate of Columbia University back on the upper east side of New York City. The structure seemed to be -- almost -- at the same angle to the sun.

Tom had taken the entrance exam at Columbia, but had not been admitted. He wanted to study literature with the French essayist, Jacque Barzun, who was teaching there.

After Tom's remark, Vern shifted the Porsche into low gear, and with his lips tight together, sped away abruptly from the campus gate.

All last night, Tom lay awake thinking he better drop the tourist-mission part of this visit to San Francisco, and start looking for a job.

But, this Sunday morning, Vern was all smiles again, and at morning coffee, said, as soon as Bliss was ready, they would all drive down to Monterey and Big Sur -- after a waffle breakfast in town.

Vern played the responsible-father role convincingly, Tom thought, but that was out here in California.

There was a different Vern, a reckless Vern, back in Detroit at Denby High School. And Tom wondered if his friend had <u>really</u> changed.

Tom knew that for an overly intelligent guy, Vern turned into a patsy when it came to women; he lost all control.

That was evident, when Tom saw him throw away his future with a car-dealership daughter of a family, who offered to buy him for her. They were both seventeen.

The car dealer family promised that Vern would never have to work, and they had a house in Boynton Beach, Florida, he and his bride could live in. All he had to do was make their daughter happy.

Vern was saved by his lawyer father, who put his foot down hard, saying his son was going to the University of Michigan, then on to law school. If a lawsuit was needed, his father told him, that could be arranged. The daughter was sent away to Bryn Mawr College in Pennsylvania.

There was another thing troubling Tom. Since his arrival at the house, he could see Bliss was drifting away from Vern, and the dope was not doing anything to stop it.

The drift did not show when they had been in Detroit for a visit, but now out here in California, Tom noticed the difference.

Tom wondered if he should tell Vern of the change he could see in Bliss -- but was it his place to say anything about it? About how Bliss seemed disenchanted with her present way of life, despite his financial and legal success.

"Well," Vern said suddenly, while folding his newspaper, "if everybody is ready -- let's hit the road."

"Just a few minutes," Bliss said wiping the baby's face, "we're almost done."

"Monterey is where Steinbeck wrote his books," Tom said, to distract Vern, delay him until Bliss was done feeding the child, and Shelly drinking what milk was left in her glass, "while he was working on a newspaper as a reporter. To see that kind of stuff -- is right up my alley."

"He wrote 'Cannery Row,' there," Vern said tapping his newspaper even on the table. "And I read somewhere, 'The Grapes of Wrath' and 'Of Mice and Men' were written there too -- it's kind of an historic place for literature freaks."

"In his biography," Tom said smiling, enjoying the talk about writing, "his writing instructors at the university told him he would be a writer 'when pigs fly' -- and suggested he stick with his newspaper job, give up trying to write fiction."

"I read about that too," Vern said grinning back, "and now Steinbeck has the face of a smiling pig -- sprouting wings -- on the last page of his published books."

They both grinned, enjoying the irony.

Bliss put the last piece of sausage in her mouth, watching the baby finish his waffle.

"We'll go to the bathroom," she said to Vern. "We'll meet you at the car."

"Okay," Vern said, "it's boots and saddles time folks," as he stood up from the table, pulling the check from under the ketchup bottle.

Bliss, holding the baby, watched as Shelly swabbed the flood of syrup on her plate with her finger, then slid off the chair.

Tom stood up, and followed Vern to the pay counter. He had enjoyed hearing the "pigs fly" anecdote again. It seemed to bolster what he was trying to do in becoming a fiction writer.

The heavy Mercedes sped through the hill country, Vern driving too fast for Tom, making him uncomfortable. Looking back to Bliss, holding the sleeping baby on her lap, and Shelly leafing through a large-paged book of ballet pictures, he felt a pang of responsibility for them.

He thought of saying something to Vern about slowing the car speed down, but only said, "Is this hill country always this brown?"

He leaned across to look at the car speedometer; they were doing almost ninety miles an hour.

"This is the fall season out here," Vern said keeping his eyes on the road. "Everything turns brown -- but the sunshine stays the same -- bright."

Finally Tom blurted, "Don't you think you should slow down a bit?"

"Ah-h," Vern said, "this car was built for Autobahn travel over in Germany -- you can drive any speed you want over there."

"I _was_ over there," Tom said, "but this ain't the Autobahn, man."

"We don't want to spend the day on the road," Vern said, "just travelling. We want to see Monterey."

When Tom looked back at the road, he saw ahead a long string of motorcycles, riding in twos in the right lane of the highway. Some had girl passengers riding in the group, that Tom quick-counted at about fifty.

When Vern began passing the motorcycles in the left lane, Tom pressed back in the car seat, as if to hide, make himself smaller. The motorcycle gang looked menacing.

One motorcycle rider glanced back at Tom as he passed in the big Mercedes, and so their eyes would not meet, Tom looked down at the spotless chrome engine.

Passing the group, everyone sat silent in the car.

Tom saw most of the cyclists had long hair, and wore leather vests and Levi's. Their arms, reaching forward for the handlebars at eye-level, were covered with tattoos of skulls and snakes, and barbed wire.

The girls riding on some of the bikes wore leather jackets with sleeves, and their tight Levi's, showed round thighs, that they pulled up to hold the driver.

As Vern drove past the lead motorcycle, Tom looked across at the driver, who wore long hair and mirror sunglasses, and who looked back.

There seemed to be mutual curiosity, but he showed no emotion while looking at Tom, as if to say, you have a life with a Mercedes, and I have my chrome motorcycle.

There were no gestures, or even a change in facial expressions from the cyclists, as the Mercedes passed them, Tom had noted.

"I hope we don't see them again," Bliss said.

"They certainly make a statement," Vern said. "Don't mess with us -- is their message -- very loud."

He eased the big car over into the right lane.

"Why do we _always_ have to pass them," Bliss said. "Whenever we see them on the highway, you always pass them," she said to Vern.

"We don't want to follow them," he said back, "to wherever we're going. Do we?"

Tom glanced back at Bliss, the picture of domestic perfection with her two children, and saw her looking out the side window of the car, as if asking for some kind of relief.

There was an impending storm, Tom thought, and by his coming to California, he stepped right into the path of it.

Seeing the road sign for Monterey, Tom began chattering to ease the tension in the car, saying, "Steinbeck wrote for a newspaper here -- and from all the reporting he did on the Oakies coming to California, he got the idea to trace their steps, back along Route Sixty-Six to the dust bowl country.

"It ended up with him writing the book 'Grapes of Wrath,' right here in Monterey."

"Huh," Tom said shaking his head, "he wrote in a garage -- his father let him live in -- use as a studio."

Vern, who knew the Steinbeck story before Tom put it into words, said, "You and your girlfriend did some 'living' in a garage back in Detroit -- I hear. Hey, kid?"

"Yeah, Tom," Bliss said from the back seat, smiling, "we heard that you two nearly wound up in court for 'gross indecency' or was it 'lewd' and that other word -- acts."

Vern's wisecrack about the sex incident had brought Bliss out of her pensive mood, Tom could see, smiling back.

"I can explain the whole incident," he said. "It was nothing like what was reported to the police."

"We're all ears, Tom," Bliss said.

"Ann Calthorp uses <u>half</u> her father's garage," he said. "Well -- it's more a garden shed than a garage -- for her studio, the place she paints her pictures.

"Her father has an herb garden that takes up almost the whole back yard, and he keeps seeds, fertilizer, hoses, and his garden tools -- there's even a sink -- back there."

"Get to the sexy part," Bliss said in a teasing tone.

"Ann has in her half of the garage," Tom said, "an old bedroom dresser with a mirror, and old couch, and two tables; she puts her painting stuff on the tables, and it's all in a mess.

"The garage, and the big house, are old, and the garage windows are up high -- just below the roof line."

Tom was silent a moment, looking out the car window at the town of Monterey and the Pacific Ocean up ahead.

"So, I thought," he said, not distracted by looking at the town, "when Ann asked me to pose for a -- life drawing -- there would be no problem."

"You mean you <u>thought</u> you had privacy," Vern said.

"Now the story is getting good," Bliss said, shifting the baby, Frederick, on her lap to a more comfortable position.

"I saw some of the paintings Ann did of herself," Tom said looking at the ocean, "they were stacked on the floor. She'd painted herself -- nude -- from the waist up -- from her reflection in the mirror on the old dresser.

"So, I thought it was okay to pose naked on an old Indian blanket on the couch."

"I understand from the report," Vern said grinning, "Ann was naked too."

"Yeah," Tom said, "I'd told her I would pose naked -- if she was naked too."

"So how did you get caught?" Bliss asked in a high-pitch voice.

"A neighbor lady was cleaning on the second floor in the house next door -- she could see down into the garden house," Tom said quietly.

"And she called the cops," Vern said laughing.

Bliss let out a <u>whoo-op</u>!

"The police report said <u>both of you</u> were on the couch, my dad told me," Vern said, "and the lady said it looked like -- you two were making love -- in public. Dad told me the whole story on the phone, after you asked for his legal help."

"Hey," Tom said, trying to act indignant, "that's client-lawyer privileged information.

"Besides, Ann was just showing me the position -- she wanted me to pose in."

Vern, driving, threw his head back for a moment, laughing.

"That's our Tom," Bliss said, smiling. "That's why we're glad you came out to California -- you'll fit in out here before you even realize it."

CHAPTER 7

In Monterey, Tom and Bliss were standing on the sidewalk next to the Mercedes, and smoking, watching Vern crossing the street, holding Shelly's hand, walking her to the Dairy Queen for ice-cream.

"Remember when I was in Detroit," Bliss said, "last year, when my mother had that operation?"

"Yeah," Tom said, watching her as she leaned to look through the car window at the baby sleeping on the back seat, her cigarette held up high, like a ballet dancer.

She spoke in an even tone, as if confessing.

"Your writer friend," she said, "the one we went to see in that carriage house --"

"That was Gary Gardner. He was typing his novel in that Indian Village carriage house; he wants to be Herman Miller number two. He only had that summer free, to type his book that ran seven-hundred pages."

"He called me at my parent's house," she said so soft Tom could barely hear her, "and we went out a -- couple of times."

"That bastard," Tom said, shocked. "But what can you expect from a farmer -- like him -- who did his undergrad studies -- at that agriculture college up in Lansing."

"He was -- very polite -- when we went out, Tom."

Over the top of the Mercedes, Tom could see Vern and his daughter, standing at the ice-cream counter.

Not looking at Bliss, deliberately, Tom said, "Lord Shaftsbury; Gardner was writing his doctorial thesis on Lord Shaftsbury, who was a friend, or patron of Shakespeare. Gardner told me when I met him at Wayne State.

"For money, he did the PR for the Athletic Department at the college, to pay his way as a doctorial candidate.

"I never figured he'd pull something like that -- you know -- hitting on a friend's wife."

"When he got serious," Bliss said, "I broke it off -- told him I'm a wife and mother -- and we better not see one another any more."

"I'll wring his neck," Tom said, dropping his cigarette, stepping on it, "the next time I see that bastard."

"It wasn't all <u>his</u> fault," Bliss said softly, while dropping her cigarette on the ground for Tom to step on.

Tom felt surprised and guilty at the same time, after hearing what Bliss told him about her and Gardner.

Surprised that Bliss went out with him in the first place; then feeling guilty for having introduced them, with Vern back in California, and Tom being trusted to shepherd her around Detroit in her husband's absence.

Watching Bliss looking at the baby again in the back of the Mercedes, Tom had a fleeting thought; maybe Gardner was just playing a Herman-Miller-in-Paris role -- in making a pass at Bliss. Maybe he was fantasizing he had to act like Miller.

He remembered too, that the family in the big house must have been impressed by Gardner's constant typing, with the window open that summer, that after several weeks, the mother sent the children to the loft, to invite him to Sunday dinner.

When Gardner told him about the dinner invitations, Tom could see the typing was leading Gardner to thinking he was a celebrity.

"Sorry I put you in that position with Gardner," Tom said to Bliss, while looking across the street, watching as Vern and his daughter came out of the ice-cream shop. "I should have known better."

"It wasn't <u>all</u> his fault," Bliss said softly.

"No," Tom said, "it was mine."

Driving in the car again, Vern pointed to a row of buildings near the waterfront in Monterey.

"Cannery row was right about there," Vern said. "It was the housing for the people who worked canning the fish over in the plant on the docks."

Tom sat silent; he did not care much about the book Steinbeck wrote about the cannery workers.

"That's the Oceanic Institute," Vern said, pointing to a cluster of glass front buildings, built up to the edge of the water. "They do all the research there, on ocean life."

Tom nodded.

When Vern turned at the corner, Tom saw the blue and white logo, "HP" on the side of a building.

"That's the company that makes the home computers," Vern said. "They're really catching on -- we have a computer in our office -- you ought to buy some of their stock -- and make some money, kid."

Tom nodded, trying to act interested.

But later, when they drove into Carmel, Tom sat up alert, looking at the view where the rust-colored cliffs ended and the sea rolled in gently. Everything seemed calm in the late afternoon sun; his mouth dropped open.

"Isn't this place something," Bliss said from the back.

"Yeah," was all Tom could say, looking at the grass that grew nearly trimmed below the tall pine trees, that overlooked the Pacific Ocean, where a soft mist rose from the waves up to the high cliffs. It was a park, but maintained by nature.

"I feel like I'm in a picture -- a natural picture," Tom said as Vern drove slowly to Big Sur. "I'm seeing where America ends at the sea -- I've never seen anything like this place before."

He was going to say the trip out here was worth the trouble to see this view, but he did not speak.

When Vern turned the big car at Big Sur, he said, "The people who live around here -- they keep this place -- pristine."

"Right," Tom said. "There's no cigarette butts, or gum wrappers. That's the way it should be."

"It almost makes you want to cry," Bliss said. "It's <u>too</u> beautiful."

Tom nodded, looking at the orange sun out over the ocean.

Vern said, "Sorry, folks," as he drove back up the road to Carmel, "But it's time to head back home."

"I'm grateful you let me see Big Sur," Tom said. "It's hard to leave here -- to stop looking. It's the kind of place that takes hold of you -- you can't get enough."

"It'll always be here," Vern said. "You can always come back to it."

"If you move out here to California, Tom," Bliss said in a cheerful tone -- almost musical, "you can come here whenever you want."

Tom nodded, thinking she was talking about something more than Big Sur, but he did not know what.

He sat silent for a moment, and the thought he has seen America from Big Sur, all the way back to Montauk, out on the tip of New York's Long Island, and he has not found a place to settle down yet.

Then he smiled, thinking Monterey sort of resembled Sag Harbor out on Long Island, but what is the sense of comparing two places.

What he needed, he told himself, was an interesting place to write his fiction stories, and as of yet he has not found one. The pressure to move away from home was forcing his hand. He felt he was stumbling around in the dark.

He would know the right place when he found it; he was certain there would come a flash of light, or bells would ring, when he found the right place.

Until then, he had to keep looking.

*   *   *   *   *

It was dark when the Mercedes' headlights light the steps back at the house in Wildcat Canyon, as Vern drove up the steep driveway.

Both children were sleeping. Vern took Shelly from the back of the car, and Bliss, holding the baby, was stepping out, Tom holding the car door open for her.

"I'll put the car in the garage," Tom said to Vern starting up the dark steps.

"I've got the car keys," Vern said from the steps as he was going up, "the house key is on the same ring."

Bliss stepped out of the car, lifting Frederick to her right shoulder, Tom watching her in the faint glow from the car interior dome light.

Her left breast brushed fully against the back of Tom's arm holding the door, as she moved past him.

Suddenly the front porch lights up above came on, then the lights on the steps; Vern had switched on the lighting inside the house after unlocking the door.

"California is beautiful," Bliss said, halting for a moment on her way up the steps. "We told you -- you would enjoy it out here."

"Yeah, you're right," Tom said slamming the car door, telling himself it was just an accident, her brushing his arm. "But I got to see the Jack London places -- while I'm out here. It's part of the obligation of one writer -- to snoop on another writer."

"Don't worry, Vern will show you everything you want to see -- when he gets time -- off from work."

As she started again up the steps, Vern came out on the landing above her, "Shelly's on her bed," he said quietly.

"I'll tuck her in," Tom heard her say, "after I put the baby in his crib."

Car headlights came up the dark driveway from down below.

"We got company," Tom shouted, then slamming the card door.

"Yeah," Vern said coming away from the steps, handing Tom the Mercedes keys, "he wants to talk shop. He's got a big decision to make."

Taking the keys, unlocking the garage door, and while walking to get in the big car, Tom heard Charlie Bellows say to Vern, "Last year I filled out an application for the Foreign Relations Department in Washington -- and, well, now I got a letter.

"They want me to come to Washington -- they have an opening to be filled."

"Come up to the house," Vern said to Charlie, "we'll talk."

When they went up the steps, Tom parked the Mercedes in the garage, and closed the door from the outside; he did not want to intrude on the two lawyers' discussion upstairs, and was going to sit on the steps and smoke a cigarette.

Walking past the Porsche parked in the shadow side of the driveway, he heard the sharp <u>crack</u> of a twig break, down in the dark of the sloping driveway.

He stopped, and slowly backed out of the light from the steps, into the row of shrubs.

"Could be an animal," he said under his breath, looking in the direction of the noise.

He waited until he felt sure of no other sound, and was about to move, when he spotted the head of a man in the dark trees behind Charlie Bellows' car.

"Somebody's on the prowl," Tom whispered to himself, watching, lowering himself down on one knee.

The figure moved to the corner of the house, and from a tall shrub, reached out and put something on the glass of the end window.

When Tom saw the arm holding up a package the size of a cereal box, he muttered softly, "That guy is making a recording -- for shit sake. What the hell has Vern got into now?"

Suddenly, Tom saw the figure remove the appliance from the window glass, duck down, and disappear into the dark.

Tom could not make out which way the intruder went.

Getting up from kneeling, Tom said, "Vern isn't going to believe this one -- when I tell him."

Standing still, trying to get a glimpse of the intruder down in the dark sloping driveway, he muttered under his breath, "He must have gone down to the road -- he'd have to."

The house front door opened, then Vern and Charlie Bellows came out.

Tom started walking up the steps, and when Vern saw him, said, "hey, man, what you doing grousing around out here in the dark?"

"You wanted me to park the bus," Tom said, flipping the ball of keys on the ring at him.

Stepping through the door, Tom stood for a moment listening.

"I guess I'll go then," he heard Charlie Bellows say, "I haven't been overwhelmed with accident clients lately.

"I'll give Washington a few years -- and if it don't work out -- and Clarissa don't like it there -- we can always move back here to California."

"You <u>may</u> like life in the capitol, Charlie," Vern said, leading the way to the top step; Tom saw when he turned slightly. "And it's <u>steady</u> work, man. Try it; take a chance on what's being offered."

"I guess I'll do that," Charlie said stepping down on the first step. "And thanks for your time, Vern -- to hear me out."

"Hey," Vern said, "maybe I'll have to come to you for advice -- in Washington. Who knows."

Grinning, Charlie said, "Thanks again," before turning to go down the steps.

Inside the house, Tom was pouring scotch into a glass, when Vern came into the sitting room.

"You had a night visitor out there -- a few minutes ago," he said, putting the bottle down. "I was going to jump him, but he ducked off before I could get close."

"Naw," Vern said pouring scotch into a glass, "it was probably a cop -- snooping around. They said they would be around -- watching."

"But this guy looked like he was recording," Tom said and sipped the scotch.

Then he said, "I think I saw him put a listening device on the window."

"C'mon, Tom," Vern said smiling, "you're imagining things -- your writer's imagination is at work here."

When Vern sat down on the couch, he said, "The guy might just be checking the window -- the view looking inside -- to see what a peeping-tom would see."

Bliss came into the sitting room.

"I'm getting a pineapple snack for the kids," she said, smoothing back her hair with both hands.

"They ate nothing but junk today -- waffles, syrup, and ice-cream. You guys want some pineapple?"

"No thanks, babe," Vern said.

"I got scotch," Tom said holding up his glass. "Thanks."

"You don't look so good, Tom," she said running her hands over his backside. "You feel okay?"

"I'm just a little tired -- all the excitement," he said looking up at her. "But the scotch will help."

"You should take better care of yourself," she said before stepping over to the kitchen door, snapping on the light.

CHAPTER 8

The next morning after the Big Sur trip, the phone rang in the kitchen while Tom was boiling an egg.

"Kyle Browning wants to welcome you to sunny California --" he said with a smile in his voice. "Vern called me from his office."

"He said you might even move out here. It's about time you get wise."

"Hey, Kyle -- you still hustling encyclopedias on the unsuspecting?"

"I only do it by appointment," he said, "and I'm going to art school on the G.I. Bill -- over in Oakland."

"You must be kidding," Tom said reaching to turn off the stove flame under the boiling pot with the egg.

"I'm learning to make Native American jewelry -- out of silver -- and it's expensive -- the cost of silver."

"How come Indian jewelry?"

"I'll tell you all that, later, when I catch up with you face-to-face. Hey, have you seen the sites around the Bay area yet?"

"No, Vern took me and the family down around Monterey yesterday."

"What are you doing this morning and today?"

"I'm just eating my breakfast -- Canadian Club and a boiled egg."

"Same old Tom -- <u>always</u> with the booze -- huh."

"All writers need a stimulus."

"Still writing -- you sold anything?"

"Right now -- I'm waiting to hear about some stuff I sent to a publishing house."

"Well -- it's better than working -- being a writer."

"You should talk."

Kyle laughed, then said, "I'll be over to pick you up in about half an hour."

"Vern said you have a Bultaco."

"No, I wore it out -- and I can't afford to take it to the repair shop -- have it fixed up. I got my wife's Volkswagen. I'm doing some -- advertising -- today. I drove her to work at school, and I got her car. Ah-h, I'll talk to you when I get over there. Okay?"

"Alright," Tom said hanging up the wall phone, then, with a wood spoon, lifted the egg out of the hot water.

He was washing his plate and cup in the sink, when Kyle knocked at the door.

"Long time no see," Tom said when they shook hands at the front door. "Or should I say -- it's been many moons."

"No ethnic slurs," Kyle said, looking around at the furnishing of the sitting room, as he followed Tom inside, while lifting his horn-rimmed glasses higher on his nose.

Tom looked at Kyle in a yellow tennis shirt, scruffy saddle shoes, and summer slacks.

"You look like you're dressed for Missus Bixby's tennis class," Tom said grinning.

"Yeah," Kyle said, "you know there are a lot of people in Grosse Pointe that don't even know -- there is a tennis club back there."

"It's behind Brownell School," Tom said grinning. "Looks like a Quonset hut."

"I went to Brownell -- when I was a kid," Kyle said. "We lived only a couple of blocks away."

He followed Tom into the kitchen.

"Sounds like you can take the boy out of Grosse Pointe, but you can't take the Grosse Pointe out of the boy, Kyle."

"Hey, Tom, how you fixed for money?"

"Well -- I -- am a little short on cash, Kyle."

"That's what I expected," Kyle said leaning on a kitchen chair back. "How would you like to make -- ten bucks today?"

"That sounds good," Tom said, "if I don't have to shoot somebody to get it."

"I'm putting up advertisements in the supermarkets today, that's why I got Doris' car," Kyle said.

"The encyclopedia company pays a buck for each of the ad flyers put up," he said, adjusting the eyeglasses up higher on his nose, slowly, as if he was speaking of some corporate funds.

"What do you want me to do?"

"You're the jumper -- we put up twenty today -- you get ten bucks. Let's get going, and I'll fill you in."

In the Volkswagen, Tom saw on the back seat piles of papers and books, and in one corner, a clear plastic raincoat all wadded up.

"Are these the flyers?" he said, taking one from the stack on the floor under his legs. He looked at the yellow card, showing a mother leaning over a young boy, leafing through an encyclopedia.

"Yep, you stick it on the bulletin board in the supermarket, just inside the front doors. You pull the old one off," Kyle said, holding up a square of cardboard with rows of thumbtacks he pulled from the pocket of the door on his side of the car. "Use one of these to hold it up."

"That's all I have to do?"

"Yeah -- I know where all the supermarkets are -- that's why I'll do the driving."

"When do I get paid?"

"Tomorrow. When I go to the office, I'll turn in a voucher for all the locations we put up a flyer," Kyle said, waiving a clipboard that had been sideways between the seats.

"They must trust you," Tom said grinning. "Sometimes -- they do spot checks."

"Okay, coach, I'm ready."

They were driving to put up the eighteenth flyer, when Kyle said, "we can zip over to the city -- if you want to see China Town -- or the cable cars -- or even the fish market on the waterfront."

"I'm more interested," Tom said, "in something like seeing Jack London's old house -- writer stuff."

"There's Johnny Heinhold's bar -- over in Alameda -- London used to hang out there."

"Hey, I'd like to see that, man. Maybe have a beer there."

"Okay. Three more flyers, and we'll buzz over there."

Johnny Heinhold's bar looked like a railroad freight car with the wheels off, set on a concrete slab that ended at the waters edge of the bay.

"It looks like it's covered with tarpaper," Tom said, as they drove up closer.

"It is tar paper," Kyle said smiling. "The inside is even worse. There's a sign in there that says Johnny introduced London to Captain Larson here -- the guy he made into the main character in his book 'The Sea Wolf.'"

"No kidding," Tom said looking at the door as they drove up. "I can't wait to go inside -- man, this is great."

Inside the bar was pitch dark, except for the lights over the bottles on the back bar. The bar itself was a low counter that ran the length of the room. In front of the counter was a line of swivel stools.

Kyle whispered, "This place reminds me of the old time lunch counters -- like they have in the movies."

"It's terrific," Tom said. "The atmosphere is terrific for a writer. Let's have a beer. This is history, man -- literary history."

He looked up at the bartender, who towered like a giant behind the low counter.

"Where did Jack London sit?" Tom asked reverently.

"There, they say," the bartender in a white shirt said in a deep voice, pointing to the second stool from the wall.

"And the captain, Wolf Larson, sat here," he said pointing to the stool in front of him.

"I want to sit on London's stool," Tom said, while moving down to near the wall, hunched, sliding over the stools between.

"Two Olympia beers," Kyle said to the bartender, moving to sit on the stool next to Tom. "He's a writer," he said, pointing a thumb at Tom.

"So this is where Jack London drank," Tom said sitting up straight on the stool. "This is a landmark."

"Not for long," the bartender said, as he set two bottles of beer on the counter in front of them. "The navy wants it moved. They say this building is in the way -- when they dock their big ships."

"Where do they want to move it to?" Tom asked, holding the beer bottle, before taking a drink.

"It hasn't been decided yet," the bartender said. "Nobody knows for sure."

"Too bad," Tom said, "this is a historic place -- they should leave it alone -- leave it just where it is."

A man and woman, both wearing sweatshirts, came into the bar and sat at the far end. The bartender moved down to serve them.

"So Johnny Heinhold was a friend of London's," Tom said looking around the room, holding out his bottle of beer.

"That's what everybody thinks," Kyle said, then taking a drink of beer. "But I read -- someplace -- that he was the only bar owner that would let London drink on the tab -- when he was ashore broke."

"London used to sail with the whaling fleet that docked here in the bay in the last century. He drank a lot -- was broke all the time," Kyle said.

"Yeah, most writers live like that," Tom said, grinning, before taking a drink of beer.

Later, when they were walking to the Volkswagen, Kyle said, "We have to hurry back -- I got to pick Doris up at three-thirty."

At the school, Tom watched as Doris came outside when she spotted the Volkswagen, walking with her pregnancy showing; she was heavy to begin with, the shape of a Swiss milkmaid, so her stomach was not too prominent.

"They want to put Kenneth back a year -- make him repeat the second grade," Doris said to Kyle, after saying hello to Tom, who had climbed into the back seat.

"How come?" Kyle said while driving away from the curb, his face showing a concern.

"They claim he's retarded," she said looking at Kyle, her eyes narrow. "He's not retarded. He's just -- over active -- hyper active -- to use their words."

"We'll talk about it later," Kyle said. "I'll drive Tom over to the Hurley's house -- and I'll come right home."

"Okay," Doris said, then turned back to look at Tom. "How long you going to stay in California?"

"Maybe a week -- maybe two," he said. "Vern has a lot of places he wants me to see."

"There's so much going on out here," Doris said, as if overwhelmed. "You'll be surprised -- there is so much happening that you can't take it all in -- you're sure to like it out here -- find something you like to do."

When Kyle drove up the cement driveway of the house on the side of a hill, Tom saw screens on the porch front windows, the building in this working class neighborhood looking more like a cottage back in Michigan, than a permanent residence for a family.

There was a faded paper notice tacked near the screen door of the house:
TERMITES

"What's the sign mean?" Tom asked.

Kyle held his finger to his lips, watching Doris slowly getting out of the car.

Tom nodded, keeping quiet.

"I'll drop Tom off -- I'll be right back," Kyle said to Doris as she closed the car door.

Tom opened the door, and moved up to sit in front again.

"You'll have to come by -- and visit us," Doris said to Tom through the open car window. "In a day or so."

She rested her hands on her stomach as she turned to go into the house.

"Yeah," Kyle said, backing the Volkswagen down the incline, looking back, "the Forty-Niners are playing Detroit -- how's that for coincidence?"

"If you want, come watch the game with us Sunday."

"We'll see, Kyle," Tom said, thinking he better not mention the 'TERMITES' sign again; it seemed to be a touchy subject.

Passing a sign that read Wildcat Canyon, Kyle suddenly shouted, making the Volkswagen lurch, "I just remembered -- they're having a 'Happening' Friday for the graduating class at the Art School. You can come as a guest."

"What's a Happening?"

"Kind of a party," Kyle said lifting his eyeglasses higher on his nose. "To celebrate -- for the winners, who took prizes in the State Art Contest."

"They're going to set-up a parachute tent over a stage -- even have a piano -- out on the grass in front of the school."

"Well," Tom said, "I have to see what Vern's got on tap for Friday."

"Sure," Kyle said. "Just let me know -- I'll give you our phone number."

In the driveway of the Hurley house, Kyle remained seated in the Volkswagen, the motor running.

"Aren't you coming in for a second?" Tom asked.

"Not today," Kyle said handing Tom a notepaper with his telephone number, "we're having meatloaf -- the whole family is home."

Tom waived, watching the Volkswagen turn around and go back down the steep driveway.

CHAPTER 9

"Do you eat Chinese food?" Vern asked Tom, as they drove on the street of Chinatown lined with shops, Bliss sitting between them in the Mercedes.

Tom was going to wisecrack, "Only when I have to," but said quietly, "Yeah, sure," to act like an appreciative houseguest.

Vern and Bliss were showing Tom San Francisco after dark, the cable cars in the hilly part, the Golden Gate Bridge all light up, and now Chinatown.

A baby-sitter, Melanie, who he could not take his eyes off of when she came to the house, stunning him with her blond hair and trim figure, was watching the children.

When he asked Bliss about Melanie, he was told she had a twenty-two year old boyfriend, and he was married.

Thinking that was a good opening to get to know her on his terms, Bliss added to the fire by telling him Melanie lived with her mother, four houses away, a divorcee, who drank a lot.

It was hard for Tom to think of anything but Melanie now, but he controlled himself enough to act like he was appreciating the tour of the city.

When they walked through the door of the Chinese restaurant with Woo Fat Noodle Company on the front window, he said to Vern, "That's an odd name for an eating place."

"It's the best around," Vern said as they were sitting down at a table in front of the window.

Bliss, smiling, said, "Their food is authentic Chinese -- you'll enjoy it."

After wonton soup, they were eating egg rolls, dipping them in plum sauce, when Vern sat back in his chair, his mouth dropping open.

"What's the matter?" Bliss asked quietly.

"Just a stomach cramp," he said softly. "I had lunch with Noel Appleton today -- we had oysters -- at the waterfront -- while we discussed business."

"You don't look good -- you're pale," Bliss whispered. "Go to the bathroom -- put cold water on your face, honey."

"That might help," he said getting up from the table, and dropping his napkin on the chair. "I'll only be a minute."

"Take your time," Bliss said up to him. "If it doesn't get better -- we'll go home."

Despite her speaking with concern, Tom had a sense she welcomed Vern's ailment at the same time. She seemed far too detached from his suffering. There was a distance between them, and Tom could not see it directly, but he could <u>feel</u> it.

When Vern was gone, Bliss asked Tom, "Have you seen the 'Bonnie and Clyde' movie yet?"

"Ah-h," Tom said dipping his morsel of egg roll in the plum sauce, swirling it, "I don't go to the movies much."

"Everybody's talking about it at school," she said, dipping her egg roll on the end of a fork, "Dunnaway and Beatty are terrific -- everybody says it's worth seeing."

Tom sat wondering for a moment, if the theater marquee, with the three-foot high letters 'Bonnie and Clyde' they passed up-town tonight, had anything to do with her interest about the movie. Or, if it was just that she was eager to see a love story.

Vern came back, and while sitting down, said, "I have to remember not to have oysters and beer for lunch -- despite Noel Appleton's urging."

"That's why Noel weighs almost three hundred pounds," Bliss said to him in a stern tone.

"You're right, babe," he said picking up his egg roll. "We'll walk some -- after we finish here. That will help -- the water on the face thing -- that helped too."

"We were talking about the 'Bonnie and Clyde' movie," Bliss said, almost as if she did not care about his ailment.

"I'm going to take you to see that flick, I promise," Vern said to her, "just as soon as I get a break in my work load."

To change the atmosphere of tension, Tom said, "Hey, I'd like to see where the hippies hang out," while lifting the metal cover off his Guy Kow chicken dish. "I'd like to see the people with flowers in their hair, Vern."

"Haight-Ashbury -- we can walk there," Vern said lifting a tea cup slowly and taking a sip, then putting it down, added, "it's almost gone now -- but there are a few die-hards still hanging around."

"Where did all the hippies go?" Tom asked spooning rice from a bowl onto his plate. "I mean -- they just didn't disappear into thin air."

"They got jobs," Bliss said, spearing one of the shrimp on her plate, "like everybody else. There was no -- other place for them to go."

"Poor hippies," Tom said.

Later walking in the dark streets, the three of them stopped to look up at the street signs at the corner of Haight and Ashbury.

"So this was the center of the universe -- for the early sixties," Tom said looking up at the narrow black and white signs.

"These painted store-fronts," Vern said, pointing to one painted blue, "those were the drug clinics.

"Doctors volunteered to work down here -- treating whatever diseases the hippie kids had."

Further up the street as they were walking, they passed a barefoot girl sitting on the curb, eating out of a can with a spoon.

Vern, walking on the outside, near the curb, whispered, when they were past her, "She's got a can of <u>dog food</u>. I saw the label on the can -- she's eating dog food."

"Ah," Tom said, walking next to Bliss with his hands in his pockets, "maybe she's just putting on a show -- putting people on -- for some money -- or pocket change."

"That's a terrible thing to see," Bliss said quietly, "no matter what she's doing it for."

There was shouting up ahead, and Tom saw a colored kid walk out into the middle of the street pointing.

"That's Baldwin," the kid shouted. "The writer guy."

A group of colored boys and girls, who had been standing in front of a brightly light music store, stepped off the curb to cross the street to look at the man.

Tom looked across at a tall Negro man in a suit, walking next to a shorter Negro man in a raincoat.

"You're Baldwin," one of the black kids shouted. "That's you -- the writer Baldwin," as the group moved closer to him.

"That's him," a girl shouted. "I've seen pictures of him, and that's him."

The tall man held out his hand, as if to keep them away.

"Burn, baby, burn," the smaller man said, holding up his fist like a prize fighter, who won fight.

When the group gathered around the two men, Tom said quietly, "They probably don't know his first name is James, and the 'Burn' thing is the title of his new book."

"Let's get out of here," Bliss said taking hold of both Tom and Vern by the arm, "I feel out of place here -- all of a sudden."

When they were walking to the parking lot for the Mercedes, Tom said, "He's a sick man -- he has cancer -- and he's dying. I read about him in a magazine. He lives in Paris. I wonder what he's doing in San Francisco?"

While Vern was paying for the parking at the attendant's shack, Tom said, "The magazine had a picture of him -- he had dark circles under both eyes -- he looked in bad shape."

"Enough," Bliss said. "I want to go home to Berkeley."

"Okay, babe," Vern said, putting his wallet in his coat pocket, then pulling Bliss against his side by the shoulders, added, "our tour of the city if over."

"I wonder," Tom said, "if you could call this Street Theater," while smiling.

* * * * *

Friday, Tom rode on the Bultaco motorcycle over to Kyle's house.

In the driveway, after sliding off the cycle, he bent down to read the TERMITE sign closely.

It read: The Marin County Housing Commission has condemned this property due to Termite infestation of the foundation timbers --

"Hey, Tom," Kyle said through the screen door above him, "what you doing down there?"

"I think the cycle gearbox is leaking -- somewhere," Tom said while standing up straight, and rubbing his hands together, as if cleaning them.

"All cycles do that," Kyle said opening the screen door, then coming down the steps. "The fluid in the trans builds up -- and they leak."

Tom had to smile when he saw Kyle was wearing a white T-shirt with dark-blue piping around the collar. It made him look like a yachtsman.

"Here's your ten bucks -- for posting the flyers," he said handing Tom a worn bill.

As Tom folded the bill to put in his pocket, he said, "Maybe you should drive -- you know where we're going."

When they roared into Oakland, Kyle pointed to the school building.

"Hey," Tom said from the passenger seat behind Kyle on the motorcycle, "it even looks like a school."

"Right," Kyle, stopping the cycle to park near the front door said, "it is and old school building. It's got a gym -- swimming pool -- and all that.

49

"The Arts Society bought it from the city -- when they built a new one -- someplace."

As they were walking in the hallway, lined with the old style steel lockers, Tom saw a sign on the bulletin board.

THE FILM NOIR GROUP PRESENTS:
Saturday Night at 8PM
"The Spanish Earth"
Directed by Ivor Joris
Narrated by Ernest Hemingway
Admission $1

"Man," Tom said stopping to look at the poster, "I've always wanted to see that movie -- and you know -- I could hear Hemingway's voice doing the narrating.

"I could hear what he <u>actually</u> sounds like -- when he talks -- not his <u>writing</u> voice."

"It starts at eight tomorrow night," Kyle said smiling. "Why don't you buzz over here -- listen to your hero speak?"

"I think I just might," Tom said.

"This way," Kyle said, pushing the brass bar handle of a metal door to open it, "the Happening is out on the other side of the school -- on the grass -- away from the street and the public eyes."

Following Kyle out the door, Tom said, "This place looks expensive."

"You bet," Kyle said, almost boasting, "we have a furnace for melting metals, blow torches -- vices and work table, and all sorts of pliers -- and files to work the silver -- a big investment.

"The biggest cost though, for the student -- is the silver we work with -- and the gem stones, like turquoise. Everybody in the class does a lot of scrounging."

When they turned the corner of the building, Tom saw people dancing on a plywood floor to the music of a band, the piano player at a grand piano -- all of them under an open red and white parachute that looked like a tent.

Most of the students were sitting in groups on the grass. Some had drinks in their hands.

"So this is a California Happening?" Tom said.

"Hi Kyle," a girl with black hair down to her waist, wearing tight Levi's and sandals said, as she walked up.

"Laura, this is Tom Kemp," Kyle said. "He's from Detroit -- he writes stories. We were pals in Detroit."

"Hello," she said. "Welcome to the Bay area."

Kyle took the plastic cup from her hand and took a sip.

"Vodka," Kyle said, handing back the cup.

"See you around, Kyle," Laura said looking away. "My boyfriend's here -- he's saving a place on the grass -- there's going to be some kind of show -- or something -- I hear. It's supposed to start any minute now.

"See you Tom," she said walking backwards.

"She's at my work table in class -- we share the table -- and we talk a lot," Kyle said.

"Is that <u>all</u> you do, Kyle? Talk?"

"Ah-h," he said, "you know how it is -- she's got an apartment -- nearby."

Suddenly, the music stopped, the piano player closed the cover over the keys. The band members walked off the bandstand.

A young man with long blond hair, wearing a light blue suit and an orange bow tie, picked up the microphone off the stand next to the piano.

"Ladies and gentleman," he said, "an exotic dance routine will now be performed by Ben Culver and Jenny Chin -- for your artistic pleasure. Please remain seated during the performance. Thank you."

Tom nudged Kyle, "Hey, I could use a beer."

"Wait until after this," Kyle said. "I want to see the show."

A record of Sinatra's 'All the Way,' began playing, and a Chinese girl stepped onto the dance floor. She was wearing a long blue robe. When she dropped the robe to the ground, the crowd gasped; she stood totally naked.

"She must be one of the life-drawing class models," Kyle whispered.

"Man," Tom said, "her body is perfect."

Then a young man came out, dropped his robe, and stood naked behind the girl.

When the couple was dancing apart from one another, twisting and turning, Kyle said, "Yeah, they must be models for the sketching class," keeping his eyes on the girl.

"They sure aren't shy," Tom said grinning.

The crowd was silent; watching as the girl suddenly stopped dancing and walked over to the grass and lay down on her back.

The young man moved over to the grass then dropped down on his knees.

He began crawling on his hands and knees toward her, and she opened her legs.

"If they're from a life-drawing class," Tom said, "I wonder how much <u>life</u> -- we're going to see."

A scratching sound stopped the record music suddenly. Then a bald man in a gray suit picked up the microphone.

"This exhibition will stop immediately," he said. "Young lady, put on your robe; the gentleman also.

"This celebration is terminated -- as of this instant. All students are to leave the school property.

"This is not the sort of entertainment that is appropriate for our students. We were totally unaware of what this day's entertainment offered."

Kyle looked at Tom, "That's the school administrator," he said grinning.

"I guessed that," Tom said. "But I'm still wondering how the 'Happening' ended," he said grinning at Kyle.

CHAPTER 10

"If we're having lasagna," Vern said to Bliss Saturday evening, "we should have a red wine -- a Burgundy."

"There's white wine," she said, while setting the table for the family dinner. "We'll make it do."

"I'll zip down to the liquor store," Vern said, then shouted to Tom, who was out in the sitting room, "come, ride with me to the store. The liquor store."

Tom, sitting on the couch, was reading the letters and cards his mother had sent from Detroit in a large manila envelope, that had arrived at home, his permanent address.

In the packet was a light-blue Veteran's Administration check in a tan envelope; Tom's disability check for the lung disease he contracted on army duty in Germany.

He slipped the check in his shirt pocket.

"Yeah, sure," Tom shouted, while sliding all the mail back in the big envelope, setting it on a side table.

"We'll take the Porsche -- the top's down," Vern said, starting for the keys on the side table near the front door.

"Daddy, I wanna go," Shelly said, following her father. "I want to go in the fast car."

He stopped, then turned to look at the child in brown corduroy overalls, walking behind him.

"Okay, honey," Vern said, picking her up.

"Don't dally," Bliss said putting candles on the table. "The lasagna will dry -- and burn -- if I leave it in the oven too long."

"Back in a flash," Vern said, carrying Shelly to the front door, Tom following.

Speeding down the driveway to the street, Shelly climbed up on the console between the seats, where she had been sitting in the narrow Porsche, to stand up, holding her father's and Tom's shoulders, smiling, her blond hair tossing in the wind.

Marin County roads ran mostly parallel to the hill, but the downhill roads, crossed the flat roads at intersections. It meant, coming down, there was a flat road you had to cross.

When Vern hit the first flat road coming down, the Porsche flew into the air, and landing on the other side, scraped the nose of the car.

"Holy smokes, Vern," Tom shouted. "Take it easy!"

"This car can take it," he shouted. "Watch."

On the next downhill crossing of a flat road, the Porsche flew into the air, and landed on all four wheels.

"Holy 'mokes," Shelly shouted, laughing.

"We might lose the kid, Vern."

"Na-a. She's used to it," he shouted. "Besides -- Bliss said 'not to dally.'"

Tom took hold of Shelly's arm to hold her in the car.

On the next cross street, the Porsche hit the flat road and catapulted out so far, the rear wheels landed before the front wheels.

"We're flying, man," Vern said, smiling wide under his shade-changing sunglasses, but not looking at Tom.

"I should have buckled my seat belt," Tom shouted back, grinning, still holding Shelly's arm.

At the liquor store, Vern was paying for the bottles of scotch, vodka, three bottles of Burgundy wine, a six-pack of Heineken Dutch beer, and the Slim-Jim meat stick Shelly was eating, when Tom felt guilty for him paying for all the liquor.

Tom pulled the Veteran's check out of his shirt pocket, and using a pen on the counter, signed it.

"It's only fifty-two bucks," he said handing it to Vern. "But it will cover <u>some</u> of the cost of my food at the house."

"Okay, Tom," Vern said taking the check.

When Tom handed him the tan envelope, Vern slid the check inside, and put it in his shirt pocket, and Tom stood looking at his face, seeing only the sunglasses with Bromide that change with the light chemically.

That was all the money Tom had, and he was shocked that Vern took it, at first. Then, thinking about it, he reasoned it was only fair to pay <u>something</u> for his living expenses.

Back at the house, Bliss said, "Noel Appleton called from his office -- don't talk too long -- the lasagna is ready."

"I can't imagine what Appleton could be calling about," Vern said, setting the cardboard box of liquor bottles on the sink counter.

He walked out to his study, and Tom heard him throw the keys on the table by the front door.

"Maybe," Tom said to Bliss, "Appleton found a pearl -- in the oysters."

"That's clever, Tom," Bliss said, lifting the baby, Frederick, up into his high chair that was between her and Vern's at the table. "Don't be cute -- it might be serious."

"Okay, okay," Tom said smiling. "But I have to wash my hands -- they're a little sweaty from the ride to the liquor store."

He stepped over to the sink and turned on the water.

"Vern <u>always</u> drives that way -- going down there," Bliss said, helping Shelly into her chair. Doesn't he sweetie?"

"I like to go fast," Shelly said, looking up at her mother.

Tom was drying his hands when Vern came back from his office.

"Noel left me tickets for a Segovia concert," he said going to the kitchen sink, taking a corkscrew out of a drawer and opening one of the bottles of Burgundy.

"His wife's mother had a heart attack; they're going to drive down to the hospital in Santa Barbara."

"Wow," Bliss said, "that was generous of Noel."

She put on padded gloves and pulled open the oven for the lasagna.

"Is there salad?" Vern asked, setting the bottle of Burgundy on the table.

"The big green bowl in the fridge," Bliss said, setting the hot platter of lasagna on a wood rack in the center of the table.

Tom sat down, and while unfolding a large red napkin, said, "Segovia is about the best Spanish guitarist alive."

"Noel was going to take his family," Vern said, "and he gave me five tickets -- the concert is tomorrow night -- Sunday."

He set the salad bowl on the table, sitting down at the same time.

"Segovia is a pretty old guy," Tom said, watching Bliss cutting the lasagna with a metal spatula, making squares for serving size. "I'm surprised he's even <u>doing</u> a tour."

"Well," Vern said, "Bliss and I are two tickets, and I'll call my guitar teacher and Tom, that's four tickets. Who should we ask for the fifth ticket?"

"How about Melanie?" Bliss said, putting a square of lasagna on Vern's plate, reaching with the spatula.

"Yeah," Vern said, smiling up at Bliss. "Tom, you can call Melanie's mother and ask if she can go -- sort of a date. How's that, man?"

Tom nodded, grinning back at Vern.

Everyone was eating, when the baby, Frederick, waiving his arms, knocked his plastic glass of milk off the tray of the high chair.

"You do that every day," Vern said sternly to the child. "Now you won't have any more milk today."

He reached down on the floor and picked up the plastic container, then set it on the table, far away from the child.

Bliss stood up, silent, took another plastic glass from the cabinet, and after pouring milk to make it a quarter full, closed the fridge, and set the container on the highchair tray in front of the child.

"He does that all the time," Shelly said to her mother, when Bliss sat back down at the table.

No one else spoke.

Tom had a sense of foreboding: there was a rift building between Bliss and Vern, the spilled milk was just the tip of the iceberg. Tom could sense the animosity growing.

Tom felt his coming to California was making their conflict worse, and he felt more out of place then ever before. What was causing the conflict; he was not sure he wanted to know.

"Maybe the kid doesn't like milk," he said to make light of the tension. "Maybe he wants wine."

Picking up his wine glass, Tom said, "Salud -- salud to Segovia -- as I'm sure Hemingway said back in nineteen thirty-seven Spain."

When everyone was sipping wine, Tom kept talking, trying to promote ease, "I'm going to Oakland tonight to see the 'Spanish Earth' flick showing at Kyle's art school.

"It's a documentary movie about the Spanish Civil War."

"I read about that movie," Bliss said. "The money it made was used to buy ambulances for the Civil War over there in Spain."

"Maybe you'd like to see it?" Vern said.

"No baby sitter," she said, setting her wine glass down slowly. "But, you can go, Vern. I've got reading to do for my class."

"Okay," Vern said, picking up his fork. "I've heard the movie is suspect -- it supported the Communists in Spain during the Civil War. But what the hell -- this is California."

"Hemingway narrates the flick," Tom said, feeling good about getting Vern and Bliss talking again, "so I get to hear what he sounds like."

"He sounded tough in that short story, 'Up In Michigan,'" Bliss said, grinning. "That rape of the waitress on the dock was a rough scene."

"Yeah," Tom said, grinning, "I read Gertrude Stein gave him hell in Paris, when she read that story.

"She used a French word, and told Hemingway that he should never write like the French word in any short story."

Bliss, who was eating lasagna, smiled.

Tom remembered Bliss had said that same thing once before. It was on a long sandy beach in Saugatuck, Michigan. She was with a guy, who was a school friend of one of Tom's friends; she was not with Vern yet. Tom was with his leggy Grosse Pointe girlfriend.

He had been reading, that afternoon, Hemingway's book of short stories. Bliss must have noticed him and made the wisecrack that she hoped the beach party that night would not turn into an Up In Michigan repeat.

Tom remembered he was amazed she had read the story; the wise crack did not sink into his thoughts.

Later at Saugatuck, when he came back from the beer store, he found the Hemingway book on a pair of white panties with a pattern of tiny roses. Thinking someone had tossed the book into the pile on the blanket of girls' clothes, made when the girls had returned to the beach after changing into bathing suits up at the bathhouse, he laughed.

And later in 1956, Tom had seen Bliss at a party again with the Saugatuck guy, Bennet Crawford, who was now a photographer's assistant for an advertising agency there in New York City.

Bliss had been to Europe on a college class trip, and had just returned, but Tom was in the army and was in New York en route to Europe, and would embark in two days on a troop ship for Germany.

Tom did not get to talk to Bliss much at the party, that included mostly people who had been to college together back in Michigan. But he did hear that Bliss was staying with Crawford at his loft.

Tom had said none of this about Bliss to Vern. How she met Vern, Tom did not know; he was away in Europe for two years.

Vern had been at the Saugatuck beach party with another girl that summer. Both were attending the University of Michigan, Tom remembered.

But when Tom came home from Europe, Vern had been going with Bliss, up to the time he was drafted and sent to California.

At the table now in Berkeley, everyone was finishing the lime sherbet, when Vern said, "C'mon Tom -- we'll call Melanie's mother, see if you got a date for Segovia."

"Melanie wanted to see Segovia," Vern said, holding his hand over the phone mouthpiece, "but her mother wants to talk to you -- her date," he said to Tom. "And I think she's been drinking," he said grinning.

"Hello, this is Tom Kemp -- I'm visiting here from Detroit."

"How old are you?"

"I'll be twenty-four in --"

"Are you horney?"

"We have an extra ticket, and we thought Melanie would like to go," Tom said grinning. "It's a shame to waste a ticket -- to see a guitarist like Segovia."

"Well," the mother said calmly, "if the Hurley's are going, I guess it's okay. She's just sixteen --"

"If you feel uncomfortable," Tom said quietly, "we can just skip the invitation."

"No, no," the mother said quickly changing her tone, "she says she wants to go -- so she can go."

"Okay," Tom said, before handing the phone back to Vern, who had been listening closely. "Here's Vern again."

"Tell Melanie to come to our house about seven-thirty, Sunday," he said. "We're all going in my car -- yes -- we should be back about eleven," he added, before hanging up the phone.

"That's that," he said to Tom. "You lucky dog."

*　*　*　*

Later that Saturday evening at the "<u>Spanish Earth</u>" film, Tom felt a cold feeling on the back of his neck.

He turned around and saw a man sitting at the rear of the gymnasium. He had set up two folding chairs on the hardwood floor, and was sitting on one, his right leg up on the other. He wore a dark suit, the coat hanging open, his posture saying, "I'm here because I have to be."

On the screen, when Tom turned back, was a view of Madrid being shelled, people running in the street. He recognized the Telephone Building in the film, where across the street, he had walked to look at the statue of the writer Cervantes.

Tom listened to Hemingway's narration in slow, measured words, of the Fascist shelling of the city, and to him, the voice seemed like a clergyman speaking.

It was a surprise to Tom, who expected Hemingway's voice would be deeper, and more cynical.

When the sensation of being watched came back, Tom turned around again. The man at the rear of the gym did not seem interested in the film. It was obvious he was watching someone.

Tom asked himself, "was it Vern being watched, or he?" He shook his head, asking himself, "but why?"

57

CHAPTER 11

Tom was sitting next to Melanie in the back of the Mercedes; Vern was driving with Bliss next to him, half turned in the front seat to talk.

"Yes, I want to go to college," Melanie was saying to Bliss's question, "and my dad promised to pay my expenses."

"He does real good with his dental practice -- and he's part owner of a lab that makes false teeth -- and bridges and stuff."

"You're lucky," Tom said. "College is expensive."

"Who's baby sitting?" Melanie asked Bliss.

"Missus Kelsey," Bliss said to her smiling, "from next door. The kids know her from the back yard."

"She used to teach Kindergarten," Melanie said, looking at Tom for a moment. "I was in her class. She's old now."

"I know," Bliss said looking at Vern, who said nothing.

"Here's my guitar teacher's house," Vern said softly, "and he must be eager to go -- that's him standing out front."

Tom looked out the side window and saw a thin young man, standing with his hands clasped together, rocking from one foot to the other.

A sign in the window of the house read: PRIVATE GUITAR LESSONS.

When Vern turned the big car next to the curb, the young man attempted to open Bliss's door, and she said, "The other side -- in back," and laughed.

The young man slipped into the back seat, and then slammed the car door hard. He was a bundle of nerves.

He looked at Melanie, and Tom saw his mouth drop open; he seemed stunned by her sleek good looks, and Tom grinned.

"David," Vern said, looking at his jittery moves in the car mirror, and grinning, "this is my wife, Bliss, next to me, and that's Melanie next to you, and the guy is Tom Kemp, our house guest from Detroit."

"Hi," Tom said, watching the young man nodding, then seeing his eyes lock on Melanie's legs showing with her short skirt pulled up.

She had put on too much perfume, and Tom was sure the scent was coming from under her skirt, and it made her even more attractive to him, just thinking about it.

He wondered what effect it would have on the nervous guitar teacher; he was watching him. Melanie was the star attraction tonight, he thought not Segovia.

While they were driving over the bridge to San Francisco, everyone sat silent, looking at the lights of the city, ahead.

Then Tom, to break the silence, asked David, "How long you been teaching guitar?"

"Almost four years," the young man said, taking a quick glance at Melanie's legs.

"Dave's a good teacher," Vern offered. "I don't get much free time for my instructions -- he gives me assignments -- for me to practice."

"Is he doing okay?" Tom asked.

"Sort-of," the young man said, raising one hand and dropping it.

Then, turning to Melanie, he blurted, "How -- old are you?"

"Fifteen and a half," she said quietly. "Almost sixteen."

"Oh man, oh-h man," David said, and looked out the car side window.

Tom saw both his knees jump.

"Melanie's our baby-sitter," Bliss said, smiling at the young man.

Tom thought of saying she had a twenty-two year old boy friend, but reconsidered, smiling, thinking David might jump out of the car.

Taking a quick look at Melanie's legs, he wondered what she would do if he put his hand on her leg.

She had him excited too.

Then, attempting to appear sophisticated, Tom said, "Segovia's pretty old."

"He's over seventy-five," David said, looking out the window. "That's really old -- for a classical guitarist."

There was silence in the car again, as they drove off the bridge into the city.

After the car was parked, Bliss and Melanie, with David, were walking ahead to the Fillmore, when Tom dropped back to walk with Vern.

"You better sit with your guitar teacher -- away from Melanie," Tom said quietly to Vern, "or we might have a classical -- incident -- with this guy."

Vern grinned.

"Speak for yourself," he said.

"Look at who's talking," Tom shot back.

"Okay, maybe you're right," Vern said nodding. "I'll make sure he doesn't sit near her."

Later in the theatre, Vern led the guitar teacher by the arm to the seat next to him. Bliss sat next to him, then Melanie, and Tom on the aisle seat.

Segovia came on the vacant stage, carrying his guitar. Tom watched him nod to the audience, then sit down on a wooden chair, a spotlight overhead. He bent his head as if listening to the instrument.

When the old man began playing, Tom whispered to Melanie, "He looks like he's carrying the whole of Spain on his shoulders."

"He's so dignified," she whispered back.

When the recital ended, the audience clapping wildly, and the lights came on, Tom said to Melanie, "Let's go backstage and see if we can meet him -- maybe shake his hand."

"Okay," she said and smiled. "That'll be cool."

Behind the curtain, Segovia still sat in the chair, and was wiping his face with a large white handkerchief, looking tired.

A middle-aged couple was talking to him in Spanish, and behind them were two women waiting their turn to talk with him.

"He looks a lot older -- up close," Melanie whispered to Tom, while pulling on his arm.

Moving close against her softness and perfume, Tom whispered, "He really puts himself into the music -- and it takes a toll on him."

After the two women moved away, Tom and Melanie stepped up to Segovia, who sat tucking the handkerchief into the breast pocket of his suit.

Tom said reverently, "Maestro, it was a privilege to hear your music -- in a live concert."

Segovia nodded, looking up at him; Tom wondered if he understood English.

"This is Melanie," Tom said, taking hold of her arm to move her forward, and he saw the Maestro's face light up.

When she offered her hand, Segovia took it, and shook hands. It was as if her attractive looks, Tom thought, brought him relief from how he felt.

"It's nice to meet you in person," Melanie said, smiling down at him, and the old man's smile became wider.

A man appeared, and when he lifted the guitar out of the old man's hands, he helped him to his feet.

"No more well-wishers, please," the man said, holding out his hand.

As Tom and Melanie walked to the edge of the stage, they met Bliss, Vern and David coming up the steps.

"They took him away," Melanie said. "He's really tired."

"When we figured out where you two went," Vern said, backing down a step, "we came back too. You reporters are quick -- on the draw."

"Geez," David said. "I really wanted to meet him."

"Maybe," Bliss said, "you will, the next time he's in town."

"Man," David said, shaking his head, then slapping both thighs with his hands.

*   *   *   *   *

Back at the house, Bliss was talking to Missus Kelsey, when Vern turned to Tom and said, "That David is a real basket case -- socially."

Tom and Melanie were standing just inside the front door.

"I'm going to walk her home," Tom said to Vern. "I'll be right back."

"Hey, don't be long," Vern said taking off his sports jacket. "We'll have a nightcap -- but tomorrow I got an early conference at the office -- a strategy conference for next month's contract talks."

"I'm practically back -- all ready," Tom said, watching Vern grin.

Walking down the dark sloping driveway, Tom put his arms around Melanie's shoulders. When she stopped, he kissed her. She pressed against him, and with her softness, told him her eagerness. She knew all there was to know; the whole evening, she knew what he was thinking.

They started walking again and she said, "I want to see you soon. When can I see you again?"

"I'm not sure, honey," Tom said quietly. "You know, I could go to jail -- you're a minor."

"I know girls at school -- who go with older guys," she said, as they started walking up the driveway to her house, her arm around Tom's waist, his arm around her shoulders.

Tom thought of saying, 'People commit suicide every day too,' but instead, said quietly, "We'll get together -- the next time you babysit at the house -- that's sure."

"But that could be a week -- even more," she said.

"I've started writing in the evenings now," he said, "and when you babysit, we can get together -- we won't be out in public -- where people can see us fooling around."

"The Hurley's know we're 'fooling around,'" she said indignantly. "Bliss is pretty smart, I catch her watching us when we're at the house."

"I don't want to make trouble for them -- while I'm staying with them. Get arrested -- or something."

They were almost up to the house, where the living room lights were shining bright.

"Even Mister Hurley -- is 'fooling around,'" she said, her disappointment forcing what she was saying. "I heard Bliss say it once on the phone -- I think she was talking to her mother."

"When was this?" Tom asked, stopping to look down at her.

"About two weeks ago. Bliss was going out for the afternoon, and I went over to the house after school to sit for her -- I heard her on the phone, talking."

Tom was shaking his head as they started up the steps to the front porch. He had to work hard not to show any emotion about what she had just said.

"Got a key?" he said, calmly.

"It's open," Melanie said. "My mother's up -- she watches the late-night stuff on television."

When she pushed open the door, a weak voice asked, "Is that you, Melanie?"

"Yes, mother."

"Bring me some ice cubes from the fridge, honey," Tom heard the mother ask. "I'm watching a John Wayne movie -- he's in Ireland."

Tom kissed Melanie, pulling her hard against himself.

"You're terrific," he whispered. "We'll work something out -- so we can be together." She was overwhelming him.

"Real soon, huh," she whispered back.

Outside, walking back down the driveway, Tom, thinking of what Melanie told him about Bliss on the phone, said, "Vern, you bastard."

*　　*　　*　　*　　*

Back at the Hurley house, Tom found Vern and Bliss sitting at the kitchen table.

She had on a tan satin robe, and he was sitting in his t-shirt and slacks, and he looked like she had interrupted his drinking.

There was an open bottle of white wine on the table, and Vern had a tulip glass in front of him.

Both their faces had a grim set, until Vern, looking up at Tom, said, "You behave yourself with Melanie?"

"That depends on what you mean by 'behave,'" Tom replied.

"She looked darling tonight," Bliss said. "Have some wine -- glasses are there in the cabinet."

While Tom was reaching for a glass, Vern said, "We were discussing a problem -- that maybe you can help solve, kiddo."

"Shoot," Tom said sitting down, pouring wine into the glass on the table.

Vern hesitated, then said, "Bliss -- is concerned --"

"I don't like being left home -- alone," Bliss interrupted, "when Vern is off -- gone away -- for a long stretch of that negotiating again."

"And the freak," Vern said, "at the patio window -- that's got us both on edge. The cops grousing around too -- that don't help the situation either."

Tom, knowing what was coming, tasted the wine's dry sensation, then said, "And how can I help?"

"We want you to stay around the house nights," Vern said, while pouring wine into his glass, "at least for the next few days -- until I get through my strategy sessions at the office."

Bliss, pulling her bathrobe tighter around her by the collar, said, "and I have the children to worry about."

Vern picked up his glass of wine, saying, "C'mon Tom, it's the only solution we can come up with -- right now."

"You say it'll only be a couple of nights?" Tom asked.

"No more than two, three days, maybe," Vern said, grinning, resting his elbows on the edge of the table. "It's not like we want to ground you -- during your stay out here."

"I'd appreciate it, Tom," Bliss said, "you'll be helping us. It's a good safety measure."

"To be honest," he said to Bliss, "I've been thinking of cutting my visit short -- heading for home. I'll show you why."

He stood up from the table, saying, "I got trouble too," and walked out to the sitting room, and came back with the large manila envelope his mother sent from Detroit.

He fished out a postcard from the envelope and handed it to Vern. It read:

> I AM BACK HOME.
> WHERE ARE YOU?
> ANN

"I'd say she wants you back home," Vern said as he passed the postcard across the table to Bliss.

"Damn," she said after reading it, then giving it back to Tom.

"I'm going to write her a letter," he said slowly, putting the postcard back in the envelope, "explaining what I'm doing out here. How my writing is part of it -- and all that."

"I want to say to you two -- I appreciate what you've done for me out here," he said, pushing the chair he had been sitting on before back under the table, not looking at either of them, "and I'd like to re-pay you."

"Hey, you're not obligated, Tom," Vern said. "We thought you needed to get out of Detroit for a while.

"A change of venue thing for you -- to see if you might like to move out here -- that's all."

"That part worked fine," Tom said, "and I can't but help like California -- but now I'm being pulled back to Detroit -- and Ann."

"Why do things -- get so complicated?" Bliss asked, smoothing back her dark hair with her hand.

"I'll write Ann a long letter, tonight," Tom said. "I'll explain why I came out here --"

Vern finished the wine in his glass, then looking at Bliss for a moment, said, "Why don't you call Ann on the phone?"

"Yeah, Tom," Bliss said looking up at him, "you can use the phone in Vern's office --"

"That sounds great," Tom said. Then holding up the large envelope by the corner, he added, "I had a thought just now -- that I'll be out here for -- at least a couple of days. So I'll do the guard duty on the house, the next two or three nights."

"Great," Vern said looking at Bliss. "And in a couple of days we'll all be free to get back to sight-seeing -- with a vengeance."

CHAPTER 12

That night Tom could not sleep; he could only hear Ann's high-pitched voice on the phone saying he had no right being out in California.

In the morning, dressing and walking to the kitchen for coffee, he found Bliss feeding the children breakfast.

"I got my Art History class today," she said. "I'll drop Frederick with Missus Kelsey -- and drive Shelly to her preschool. I'll be gone -- two, maybe three hours."

"I wish Melanie could babysit during the day," Tom said while reaching for a cup. He was teasing Bliss.

"She's in high school, you monster -- she can only come nights -- to babysit." She was smiling, holding her coffee cup. "You're terrible, Tom -- you after a young girl like Melanie."

"I can always dream," Tom said, pouring coffee, then sitting down at the table opposite her.

"Momma," Shelly said, "I got to go -- to the bathroom."

"Go ahead, honey. Momma's not ready to go yet."

After watching the child slide off her chair, and walk out of the kitchen, Bliss put her cup slowly on its saucer.

"Don't tell this to Vern," she said, softly, "but there's a young man -- eighteen or so -- in my school -- that brings me a red, long-stem rose -- every day I'm there.

"He brings it to the table in the cafeteria, and says, 'You're the most beautiful woman -- I've ever seen,' and goes away," she said smiling. "I think he's an art student."

"What do you do with the rose?" Tom asked before sipping coffee.

"Is that <u>all</u> you got to say, Tom?" she said making a fake scowl. "He's so sweet."

"I could say, be careful!"

"Okay, I throw it out the car window before I get home," she said. "And I thought you writers were sensitive, Tom."

"If I were sensitive -- I'd break his neck," he said, as Shelly came back from the bathroom, pulling on her sweater.

Bliss stood up from her chair, saying, "Oh-h you, he's just a kid."

Then lifting the baby out of the high chair, she said, "We have to go -- we don't want to be late -- do we Shelly."

"I need a pick-me-up in this coffee," Tom said, looking at the cup he was holding in front of his face.

"There's Canadian Club in the cabinet," Bliss said wiping the baby's mouth with her hand.

"You won't say anything to Vern?"

Shaking his head, getting to his feet for the Canadian Club, Tom said quietly to her, "You didn't have to ask me that."

He felt like asking her why she was taking a damn Art History class -- in the first place.

The wall phone rang as Bliss was walking to the kitchen door, and she turned to reach for it.

"Oh, hello Kyle," she said grinning. "Yes -- he's here. How's Doris getting along?"

There was a pause.

"Glad to hear that," she said urgently, "but I have to run -- I've got a class."

She held out the phone to Tom, who was setting the bottle of whiskey down on the sink.

"You're up early," Tom said to Kyle and stopped, waiving back to Bliss and the children, leaving the kitchen.

Listening again to Kyle, he then asked, "What kind of job?" He grinned, repeating "Ten bucks -- for two hours. Yes, I have a white shirt and tie."

Tom heard the front door close, when Bliss and the children went out.

"I'm not going to sell Encyclopedias, am I Kyle?" Tom asked, reaching for the Canadian Club bottle, the coiled phone cord stretching. "You'll fill me in -- when I get there on the Bultaco. Okay, I'll shave."

As Tom ran the Bultaco up the steep driveway to Kyle's house, he saw him sitting on the front steps, wearing a tan suit, and winged-tip shoes, his legs crossed, and the sole of the shoe showing had a ware-hole.

"The State Department is making a film in the neighborhood over near the Art School," Kyle said standing up. "It's supposed to show typical life in America -- they're going to show it in our embassies -- to foreigners.

"They need extras for a crowd scene at a wedding. The notice was on the bulleting board -- ten bucks."

"You mean I'm going to be in a movie?" said Tom, standing, holding the motorcycle upright by the handlebars.

"If we get there on time," Kyle said buttoning his suit coat. "Let me drive -- you ride in back."

Tom saw the film crew trucks parked in front of a colonial house, two-stories high, and a wide front porch that was covered by a sloping roof, when he and Kyle drove up on the motorcycle.

On the long stretch of grass down to the road, he could see a group of young men and women dressed in Sunday clothes, gathered around a man wearing all black, waiving his arms, standing in front of a film camera on a tripod.

Kyle parked the motorcycle off to the side, behind reflectors and bright lights shining on the porch, and they both climbed off.

A woman carrying a clipboard walked up to them.

"We're here for work as extras," Kyle said, pulling down on his suit coat in front.

"Give me your names," she said. After writing, she pointed with her pen at the man in the black shirt. "The director will tell you what he wants you to do. That's him over there."

Crossing the grass to the camera, Tom said, "Man, the sun's getting warm out here."

"I hope this don't take too long," Kyle said, walking with his hands in both coat pockets to pull out wrinkles. "Laura wants to buy a used car this afternoon. She wants me to go with her."

Tom looked at Kyle, and while pulling down on the front of his sports jacket, grinning, said, "You dog -- you're asking for trouble. Women trouble."

"When ever I have 'women trouble,'" he said pushing up his horn-rimmed glasses on his nose, higher, "I just give them a good horse-humping -- you know -- putting all yourself into it. And that keeps them quiet -- for about a week -- I find."

"I told you -- you were a dog," Tom said, as they walked up to where the director was standing in front of the crowd of extras.

The director shouted to the crowd, that when the bride and groom came out of the house door, the camera would start filming, and he wanted everyone to cheer and act excited.

"I want to get this scene on film the first time we do it," the director shouted. "It costs a lot of money -- and time -- to have to film it over again.

"So -- everyone act as if they were at a _real_ wedding."

There was a large bag of rice near the camera, and everyone was to take a handful, and toss it at the wedding couple as they came off the porch.

When the film take was over, the director thanked the extras, and instructed them to step over to the table next to the trucks for their payment checks.

Sitting at the table, writing checks, was the woman with the clipboard, who took their names, Tom saw, while following the crowd.

"How much gas you got in the Bultaco?" Kyle asked when they were standing in line to be paid.

"Not much," Tom said. "I need this ten bucks bad."

"I want you to drop me off at Laura's apartment house. Okay?"

Tom, smiling, nodded.

"You like young stuff -- like Laura?"

"Me? Some of the kids at art school know Melanie. I hear you took her to see Segovia. Man, that's _real_ young, Tom. You keep it up, and you'll wind up like Fatty Arbuckle in San Quenton prison."

Looking away from Kyle, Tom saw it was his turn to be paid next.

"Tom Kemp, at your service, mam,"

When the secretary handed Tom the check, he saw it was only five dollars.

"You made a mistake," he said to her. "We were told the payment was for ten dollars. We came here all the way from Berkeley."

"Tom, don't start trouble," Kyle said quietly from behind him, "and I don't like being embarrassed, man."

"All right," the secretary said, then began writing a second five-dollar check.

When she handed it to Tom, she said evenly, "You'll never work on another film -- I'll see to that."

Tom pointed to Kyle, "He's ten dollars also -- we rode over here together."

When Kyle received his ten-dollar payment, he folded the check, and while slipping it into his coat pocket, said to Tom, "Let's get the hell out of here, man."

"I need it more than Uncle Sam does," Tom said as he followed Kyle to the motorcycle. "Besides, he can afford it."

"Tom, you can be a prick sometimes."

"Yeah," Tom said grinning. "Look who's talking, man."

"Well, no one's perfect," Kyle said, holding the motorcycle straight, closing the kick-stand up with his toe, "and you know what I mean."

*   *   *   *

Vern called home the next day, saying he and his office staff were flying to Sacramento to meet with State Mediators, and that he would be home for dinner, the following day.

Bliss asked Tom to take her to see the movie <u>Bonnie and Clyde</u> over in San Francisco, and he said yes. They went that night.

At the movie, he had fallen asleep at the scene where the couple was buying gas for the car, talking to an ugly kid, who had a mouth as wide as a letter box. They were asking the ugly kid to join them in robbing banks.

But Tom woke up in time for the scene, in slow motion, where the Sheriff and his men, ambush the couple in their parked car, riddling them with machine gun fire, killing them.

Bliss was dabbing her eyes.

"That was a real sad ending," she said, as they were getting out of their seats.

Walking up the aisle, she added, "No wonder people are saying it's a terrific movie. You hate to see them killed that way."

"It's a takeoff," Tom said as they walked through the lobby of the theatre, "on the Romeo and Juliet theme."

"Ah-h, Tom, do you writers <u>always</u> have to be so -- analytical -- so hard boiled? Can't you just enjoy the story?"

"We couldn't write," he said as they walked out of the doors to the street, "if we weren't 'hard boiled.' We see differently from people -- we put events together, that move people's emotions. We have to string the stuff into a story."

"Don't be so superior," she said bumping against him.

"Where can we get a drink?" Tom said smiling, feeling a bit self conscious, wanting to drop the writing talk; he never liked to talk about writing to people.

He felt he should keep his opinions to himself, letting his feelings show in his stories, rather than talking them away.

"I don't know the bars over here in the city --" Bliss said looking up the street.

"I've heard about a place called STEPPENWOLF out here," Tom said looking up the street in the opposite direction.

"Yeah," Bliss said, "that's an artist and hippy hangout -- I've heard about it too."

"I read the book by Herman Hesse," Tom said, shaking his head, "and man, that's a real sophisticated name for a bar -- even out here in California.

"The owner must know literature -- to name the place after a book."

"I think I might know where it is," Bliss said as they began walking to the Mercedes in the parking lot. "We can't stay too long -- Melanie has school tomorrow -- she would go home by eleven."

After they found the bar, and were sitting at a table, Tom thought while looking around, the only thing remarkable about the STEPPENWOLF is the name.

The place looked to him, like any other bar, tables and a long bar along the wall. And the people, surprisingly, did not <u>look</u> like artists.

Then, a young man and woman, passing in the aisle way next to Tom, suddenly stopped.

"You're Vern Hurley's wife, aren't you?" the man said to Bliss. "You came to the airfield -- with him the day he signed up for the flight school ground-training class."

"Oh yes," Bliss said smiling up at him, "you're the instructor for that flight school -- I remember. Why don't you join us," she said leaning back in her chair.

"We were just leaving," the man said looking at the woman with him, "but I guess -- we have time for one more."

Pulling back a chair for the woman, he said, "This is Deborah, my wife," and as she sat down, he moved out the chair next to her, and sitting, said, "Tell Vern we got the plane all fixed up again -- so he can come back to the field for the rest of his lessons."

"Yes, I'll tell him," Bliss said, acting polite. "But he's awfully tied up at his office -- right now. Your name is Kevin -- isn't it?"

After the waitress appeared, and they all ordered drinks, Bliss introduced Tom, who added, "I'm an old family friend -- visiting from Detroit."

Then he blurted, "What was wrong with the plane?"

"Oh-h," Bliss said, "my tummy is -- churning." Then in a soft voice to Deborah, asked, "Will you come to the bathroom with me -- I don't know this place?"

"Sure," Deborah said, then getting to her feet.

Kevin, watching the women go, lifting his glass of beer slowly, then looking back at Tom, said, "Ah-h -- Vern did a ground-loop -- on take off -- put our Cessna right over on its back. We found there wasn't much damage, though -- once we got it righted. And it was covered by insurance."

Tom smiled wide, while lifting his rum and coke.

"Vern never mentioned anything about taking flying lessons," he said slowly to Kevin. "He's learning everything these days -- guitar -- flying. I wonder what's next?"

He was going to add skydiving, but sipped his drink instead.

"He told me," Kevin said, "he wants to learn to fly, so he can buzz up to Squaw Valley on weekends for the skiing. He did real good in ground school," he said looking concerned in the direction of the restrooms, then added, "he's a fast learner."

When the two women came back to the table, Bliss, standing over Tom, said, "I think we should get going for home -- it's getting late."

"Us too," Kevin said overhearing Bliss. "We have a lot of cleaning up to do at our place at the airfield. We have to get there early."

They all filed to the cashier counter near the front door together, Tom, gulping down Bliss's drink of white wine while getting to his feet.

In the Mercedes, as Tom was driving, he said, "Hey, Bliss, I didn't see any poet-types in the bar, or people who looked like painters. I expected to see a lot of artists hanging around."

"You can go back some other time," she said, "and hang around -- when you don't have an old married lady in tow."

"You're not old."

"You know what I mean." Then she said looking over at him, "I had an odd feeling, I think that ending of Bonnie and Clyde affected me somehow. I had a strange sensation it was Vern and I -- getting shot."

There was a silence in the car, as they drove across the bridge back to Berkeley; Tom had let Bliss's comment pass. He did not want to hear about her and Vern's problems.

After a pause, Tom said, "Ground loop."

"What?" Bliss asked, squinting.

"I didn't know Vern was taking flying lessons," he said. "I mean, he never mentioned it."

"He's involved in so many things," Bliss said, "it must have slipped his mind. He does everything he can -- when he gets free from his work load."

"Yeah," Tom said, "but he's got the <u>money</u> -- to do things. He's lucky that way. Most people -- aren't that lucky. Me included."

At the house, when Tom stopped the car in front of the garage door, Bliss, stepping out to go up the front steps, turned, and said, "Take the car and drive Melanie home -- if you want."

"No," he said, looking up at her face, lighted by the inside car dome light, seeing her expression was drawn, full of consternation, he knew something was upsetting her deeply, but only added, "I'll walk her home."

"I'll tell her," Bliss said, and closed the car door.

Tom drove the big Mercedes into the garage, concerned that Bliss's problem involved Vern, and he did not want to be in the middle.

"I come all the way out to California," he said to himself as he climbed out of the car, "to get <u>involved</u> in family trouble. Damn."

Upstairs, Melanie was pulling on her jacket, when Tom came through the door from the garage.

"I'll walk you to your house," he said squeezing her arm.

"You better not," she whispered back.

"How come?"

"My mom's got a pistol," she whispered to the side of his face.

"Why has she got a gun?" Tom asked quietly.

"She saw a guy the other night -- walking in the woods -- when she took out the garbage to the can in back of the house."

"Melanie," Bliss shouted from the sitting room. "You better get home -- your mother will be expecting you."

"We're just going," Melanie shouted back. "Good night."

Closing the front door, Tom said as they started down the front steps, "I'll just walk you to your driveway. I'll stay down on the road -- I won't go up to the house."

"We got to be careful, Tom."

"Where -- did she get a gun?"

"It's my dad's. He was in the Air Force over in Korea -- after he graduated from college."

"He fixed teeth for them -- for two years," she said at the road, where they turned off the dark driveway, heading for her house.

"I think they gave him the pistol over there in Korea."

When Tom put his arm around Melanie's shoulders, he could feel she was tense, as they were walking.

He kissed her, standing at the bottom of the driveway up to her house, and when he tried again, she moved away from him.

"If the cops come and find her," Melanie said, back stepping up the driveway, "they'll arrest her -- find out she's been drinking -- and has a gun -- if she shoots at something. Stay here -- please," she said, and ran up the dark driveway slope.

Then Tom heard her shout, "Mom, it's me Melanie -- I'm home!"

CHAPTER 13

Bliss was sitting at the kitchen table, when Tom came back to the house after walking Melanie home. There was a half-full bottle of white wine in front of her.

"You got Melanie home pretty quick," she said. "Is everything all right?"

"Her mother was at the front door -- waiting," he said, not wanting to say too much -- it might lead to telling her about the man in the woods -- or the gun.

"Okay, that explains <u>everything</u>, Tom," she said grinning. She slid the wine bottle toward him on the table, "Here, have a nightcap -- it'll settle your nerves."

He could see the wine was relaxing her; her speech was slightly slurred.

"I need something stronger."

"There might be some Canadian Club left -- it's in the cabinet."

Tom poured what was left in the bottle into a tall glass, then sat back down at the table across from Bliss, knowing she was waiting to unload what was on her mind.

She was wearing the same pantsuit she wore to the movie.

"Hey," she said, trying to act casual, "have you visited with Carl Heminger -- yet? He's married to an English girl out here now. She was one of his customers -- at that garage he has."

Since coming to California, Tom had been <u>avoiding</u> seeing Carl, who he knew as a kid, grew up with; they lived three houses away from each other. Both had attended the same Catholic grade school, but later, Carl went to a private Catholic High School, and Tom went to public school at Denby.

Carl's father was a minor executive with a large construction company. The father always bought a Buick, explaining that a Cadillac would be too showy in the neighborhood.

Tom was not sure, it could have been his wry sense of humor, but after Carl told Tom's father that his son was drinking excessively, Tom would have nothing to do with him.

Carl quit the University of Michigan, dropping out the second year, and bought an Austin-Healy, doing all the mechanical repairs himself, Tom heard, after Carl was drafted into the army.

After army service, Carl returned to Detroit, but moved back to California, where he had served in the army and opened a repair garage for foreign cars with a loan borrowed from his father.

Vern became a customer of Carl's with his first Porsche, an older model in need of constant repair, and the two discovered they were both from Detroit, while talking, and that they knew Tom Kemp.

Tom later heard Carl's father, a mason, told his son he would be cut out of his will if he did not marry soon, settle down, and start a family.

Carl had been going with the English lady, Pamela, who was three years older than him, and when she became pregnant, they bought a new house in a subdivision of Walnut Creek.

But later, Tom had something more devastating happen to him, because of Carl's comment about his drinking.

Tom was living at home, writing fiction stories, while attending classes at Wayne State University in Detroit, when he met the "leggy" Grosse Pointe girl.

She had come home from an up-state college in New York, her father on his deathbed after a heart attack, to be with the family on a deathwatch.

But as the father clung to life, the "leggy" girl decided to take classes, get her degree that was near completion, and enrolled at the same college as Tom.

They met in a Contemporary American Literature class and began seeing a lot of one another.

A month later, Carl Heminger's father came over to Tom's house, asking his mother, while Tom was attending classes, if he would ride with him up to Houghton Lake -- to help him close up the cottage for the winter.

At first, Tom was shocked. He did not have much to do with Carl's father, the whole time he knew him. He could not understand the request -- and sensed something was fishy.

But he said he <u>would</u> ride up to the cottage, help close it for the winter.

It was autumn; brown and yellow leaves covering the ground, when they arrived at sundown at the cottage.

Tom sat at the table, looking around the room of the cottage made of concrete blocks, he was in the one large open room on one side of the kitchen, the other side the sitting room with a tweed couch and stuffed chairs in front of a fireplace.

Mister Heminger brought out a bottle of Cutty Sark scotch and a bowl of ice, and set them on the table.

He had a short drink, then went into one of the two bedrooms at the back of the house, and came out with sheets and covered the couch and chairs.

Tom sat drinking, watching as Mister Heminger reached into the fireplace to close the damper in the chimney.

When Tom asked if he could help with anything, Mister Heminger told him not right now.

After Tom had two large drinks, he watched as Mister Heminger filled his glass half-full with scotch before putting in more ice. Mister Heminger had a small drink.

By ten o'clock, Tom was getting drowsy from the scotch, and began nodding.

Mister Heminger told Tom to take the bedroom on the left when he gets tired, then poured him another half-glass of scotch, before saying he was going outside to put the lawn furniture in the garage.

When Tom insisted he wanted to help, and tried getting up on his feet, he nearly fell. Mister Heminger said there was no need for help. The furniture was lightweight plastic chairs and tables.

The next morning, Tom smelled bacon frying, when he woke up. He dressed, and walked out of the bedroom to see Mister Heminger at the stove, who turned and asked how he wanted his eggs fried.

The scotch bottle was still on the table, and after Tom poured some into his coffee, he checked how much was left, and saw that less than a quarter bottle remained.

While they were eating breakfast, Mister Heminger said they would be heading for home after he drained the water pipes.

Tom washed the breakfast dishes, while Mister Heminger was outside working on draining the pipes, and when he was finished with the dishes, he went outside.

It was a bright autumn morning; the dry leaves making a rattling sound in the wind, falling on the ground, and on the small lake down below.

From the top of the long flight of steps that lead down to the lake, Tom could see Mister Heminger, below, near a low hut, that must be the pump house for the water up to the cabin.

When Tom started down the steps, Mister Heminger shouted up, there was no need to come down, the pipes were drained.

Later with Tom, watching him lock the door of the cabin, Mister Heminger said now the place was set for the winter snows. He said too, that he liked to do things himself, be sure they were done.

Tom remembered he felt like asking what the hell he had to come along for -- then realized Mister Heminger brought him to watch his drinking. He had been sandbagged.

Now, Tom sitting opposite Bliss, said, "I don't have time to make a special trip to -- see Carl."

Bliss nodded, as if understanding.

"What did you think of the Bonnie and Clyde movie?"

"Beatty chewing on a match," Tom said, turning his glass of whiskey "didn't make him look much like an Okie."

"If only Bonnie died," Bliss said, "separate from Clyde -- I don't think I would feel so bad about them. But when they get shot to pieces -- together - it was so sad. There's something about a couple dying together -- that makes me upset."

"That's pretty perceptive, Bliss. That's even beyond the Romeo and Juliet thing."

"I just believe -- that when a man and a woman," she said looking up at the ceiling, "have something going -- they love one another -- they shouldn't die.

"Because -- they are just beginning -- and if they die -- it's a big waste. The whole world loses."

"You know Bliss, I think you are going to start writing poetry some day soon," Tom said lifting his glass to her, "I can see it coming."

"Uh-huh," she said. "Maybe," and took a sip of wine.

"Now, Tom," she said wiping her lips, "tell me what happened between you and that leggy Grosse Pointe girl. I mean, why did you break up -- really?"

"I'm not sure," he said, not looking at her, "but either it was the drinking -- or it was pressure from her father."

He thought a moment, "Or it could be both."

"How both, Tom?"

"Well," he said, moving in his seat and stretching his shoulder, "her father could have fixed it, so she would meet some new guy, or he could have checked me out -- and told her I was a bad risk -- for marriage; the drinking thing.

"Me wanting to write stores -- being dirt poor -- didn't help things either. Her old man had a picture of a starving poet in a loft -- writing by candle light, holding an umbrella over his head, the rain leaking through the roof, on the wall of his study at home."

"How did she meet this other guy, Tom?"

"I'm not sure -- it's sort of complicated now -- but I think I was being investigated -- or at least being watched," he said, looking at his glass of whiskey, thinking of Mister Heminger.

"I think -- the guy who did the investigating -- took an interest in her -- and when he knew we were having trouble, on top of her father working to get rid of me -- he stepped in and took her away from me."

"Why were you being investigated? What made you think that, Tom?"

"Maybe for the lung disease -- I caught in the army over in Germany," he said, rubbing his forehead. "Maybe I spread it around -- something like that. And -- maybe the army thinks I did it deliberately.

"The army might even think I was some sort of germ-spreading spy, maybe. I'm not sure, but the army thinks everybody is a spy."

"And you <u>think</u> the army had something to do with -- taking the leggy girl away from you?"

"If not the army -- whoever does investigations, maybe," he shrugged. "He showed up at the right time -- it's not contretemps."

"What is a contr-temp?"

"Coincidence," Tom said, leaning back in his chair.

"Okay," Bliss said, leaning her elbows on the table, "but what did the leggy girl say in all this? What was her reaction to all this?"

"She didn't know anything about the investigation thing -- that they were trying every which way -- to bust my hump.

"They guy shows up at the university -- out of nowhere -- and bingo -- they're engaged."

"So you two were separated for good? Is that it?"

"No, she broke the engagement off, and we were back together for a short while -- until --"

"Unit what, Tom?"

"The mystery man came back -- and asked her to be his wife," he said, putting his elbows on the table, leaning forward. "She told me -- when he offered her a wedding ring -- he even cried -- so she was hooked -- emotionally.

"He had a job -- I still had a term to go, before I could get my degree. So that was that."

"That's a sad story, Tom."

"The mystery man was sitting in the front room," Tom said quietly, "the last date she and I had, and we came home through the back kitchen door into the house -- her mother and sister were all upset -- they wanted me to leave."

"I can see why," Bliss said, nodding.

Tom lifted the tall glass of whiskey and said, "Now you have the whole picture -- as I can tell it. But -- there are still all kinds of questions about what went on -- behind the scenes."

"I can see why you think that, Tom," Bliss said, moving her head to one side, "but I have a mystery too -- I'm trying to find out -- if my husband -- is seeing other women."

Tom suspected she was working up to saying what was bothering her; there it was, the unfaithful husband story.

At first, he did not want to take sides, until this family conflict came out into the open. Now he felt remorse for coming to California, for taking up Vern's offer; he had stepped right into this marital trouble.

He thought a moment, then said, "What makes you think that?"

"He's away from home <u>too</u> <u>much</u>," Bliss said, raising her hands to hold both sides of her face. "When a man is out -- away from home a lot -- he has all the opportunity -- to fool around with other women."

Tom nodded, and said quietly, "But that's his work." He watched her face for a reaction, and added, "He has to travel -- to the places that involve his work. He can't do it any other way."

"I know, I know all that," she said biting her lower lip, "but I'm tired of it. He's just away too much."

Tom nodded, puffing his cheeks, blowing air.

"I even took a damn class at the college in Oakland to get myself out of the house -- see if that would help, but it's not working. I still feel -- uncertain."

He could see, no matter what he said, he was not helping, so to reconcile, he asked, "Have you said anything about this to Vern? Maybe you two could work out some kind --"

"At my Art History class," she said, as if she had not heard what he said, "I met a Negro girl who invited me to her new church. The minister is a white guy named Jones. It's some kind of 'peoples' church, open to everybody -- they even have a mission down in South America -- the jungle, and everybody can go there."

Tom sat back in his chair, not interrupting, listening.

"After religious services, my Negro friend, Caroline, said there is a side room at the church, where there's music and dancing -- and everybody gets friendly. She taught me to do a new slide-dance step; we practice it in the cafeteria at the school in Oakland sometimes."

"Are you saying," Tom asked leaning forward, "you're going to join this church?"

"Uh-huh -- the minister, Jones, is supposed to be real charismatic," she said smiling. "He can really get people excited. Caroline showed me a picture of Jones -- he wears those sunglasses like Vern's, that change from light to dark with the sunlight."

"The school cafeteria," Tom said, his reporter's instinct working, "isn't that where the guy brings you the rose?"

"Uh-huh -- he's so charming -- he makes me blush, sometimes. He's a Negro too."

"I see," Tom said, getting up from the table, having heard enough. "Vern should be home tomorrow. You can hash over your joining that church with him."

"I've got to do <u>something</u>," she said looking up at him. "This being home -- alone -- is crushing me. I can't help wondering -- what Vern's doing out there -- when he's gone for days."

"Well," Tom said, pushing his chair under the kitchen table, "tomorrow you can tell him, what you told me -- how you feel. But right now," he said, feeling he heard enough and needed to get away, "I'm on house guard duty.

"I'm going out for a smoke on the patio -- take a look around."

Bliss, smiling, getting up and pushing in her chair, said, "The children are sleeping -- I've got time to take a long hot shower -- and wash my troubles away."

Tom walked out on the dark patio, and sat on the low wall, smoking, looking around at the bushes and trees.

Down below, on the road under the drop off, a car drove past, lighting the trees for a moment with background light, and he saw nothing in the bushes.

Dropping his cigarette, stepping on it, he muttered, "<u>All Quiet On The Western Front</u> for now," and turned to go back into the house.

In the hallway, he walked past Shelly's room, next to the sitting room, then passing the master bedroom to the left on his way to his room, saw the door open, a pair of sheer, black panties lying on the floor next to the bed, and heard the shower running.

He walked quietly, the baby Frederick's crib was against the hallway wall in the master bedroom. When he was in his room at the end of the hall, he closed the door quietly.

Pulling off his golf shirt over his head, he said to himself, "I wonder if it was <u>her</u>, on the beach in Saugatuck, who put my Hemingway book on those panties with the tiny roses?"

CHAPTER 14

The next morning, after Tom showered and dressed, he walked out to the kitchen. Bliss and the children were gone for the day.

The pineapple in the fridge was probably for dinner that evening, so not knowing for sure, he only ate two slices.

From the one box of cereal on the kitchen table, that was not empty, he filled a bowl.

"Fruit Loops," he said, looking at the label, shrugging.

Then looking at the cereal, he said, "I could use a drink." Up in the cabinet, there was Vermouth, the only bottle there, and he added, "this will <u>have</u> to do -- that happens when you're too lazy to boil an egg."

He poured the Vermouth on the cereal and ate it quickly.

Stepping up to the wall phone, he called Kyle, but no one answered.

"Damn," he said, hanging up the phone, "I'm flat broke. I thought Kyle might want to go to the horse track -- we might make a few bucks. I don't even have gas money for the Bultaco -- and it's damn near dry."

Looking around the kitchen, he found where Bliss kept small change in a ceramic strawberry on a ledge over the sink.

"A dollar twenty-eight cents," he said after counting, then scooping up the coins.

Outside, the sun was warm, and he was smiling, when he turned the Bultaco into the gas station in downtown Berkeley.

While putting gas in the tank, he looked across the street, seeing the brick building with a sign: LIBRARY.

He drove over to the library and parked the motorcycle, and while going up the steps, said, "One thing about a library -- is that it's free. What more could a bum ask for? I spend so much time in libraries -- they're like a second home."

From the rows of publications on the shelves about Jack London in the Biography Section, he took down a large book of photographs.

Sitting down at a table, turning pages, he found a picture of the cabin London lived in at Dawson Creek in the Yukon. His initials were burned into a wood ceiling beam.

"He was broke too," Tom said to himself, turning the pages. "It seems to be one of the requirements -- for being a writer."

He came to a picture of the SNARK, the boat London and his second wife sailed on their tour of islands in the South Pacific.

Then he read the cutline under the picture, that said in 1908 an earthquake hit San Francisco, just as the auxiliary engine was being installed in the forty-foot sloop, but the boat escaped being damaged.

On another page, Tom found the picture of London's ruined "Wolf House" in Sonoma, made of natural stones and timbers.

It was London's mansion, burned just as it was almost completed. Tom saw the second floor was charred away, the stone chimney standing alone in the bushes overgrowing the foundation.

"London seems to have bad luck," Tom said to himself. "No matter what he did, trouble followed him. Or -- maybe that's just a writer's luck."

Tom looked at the picture of the cottage London lived in, there in the Sonoma Valley, while the "Wolf House" was being built.

The cottage had a screened-in porch, where he slept.

Another photo showed the inside of the porch, his bed, and a nightstand.

On the nightstand was the tablet, where he calculated how much morphine he needed to take for his suicide, still showing on the page.

Tom read the article under the photos, stating the fire at the "Wolf House" was speculated to have been caused by spontaneous combustion. The oily rags the workmen used to wipe down the natural timbers in the house, thrown into a pile in a corner, combusted, setting off the fire that destroyed the building.

"That sounds fishy," Tom said closing the large book.

Leaning back in the chair, he looked up at the wall clock.

"Cripe, it's almost three -- I better head back home."

As he drove the Bultaco up the driveway hill, Tom saw the Porsche parked at the bottom of the steps, the Mercedes behind.

"Yep," he said, "the gang's all here again."

Vern and Bliss were sitting on the couch in the sunroom, his suit coat draped on one corner, drinking martinis.

"Hey, sluggo," he said, as Tom walked in, seeing he was slightly drunk. "We were just talking over our schedule for the next couple of days.

"Have a seat -- bring a glass -- over there are the martini glasses."

"Were you at Kyle's?" Bliss asked as Tom turned to get a glass.

"No," Tom said carrying the glass from the cabinet, "I was at the library in Berkeley -- researching Jack London."

"Library?" Vern said, leaning forward over the low table in front of the couch, pouring Tom a martini. "That sounds like a quiet afternoon."

"I'm tapped out," Tom said looking at the martini, as Vern set the metal shaker back down on the table.

"Yeah, I had to borrow a dollar twenty-eight from the strawberry over the sink -- just to go to the library."

Bliss laughed, saying, "That's just change I find in pockets when I do the washing. You're welcome to it."

"The Bultaco was running on empty," Tom said taking a sip of martini. "It was an act of desperation to swipe it."

Tom, while sitting down in an overstuffed chair opposite them, thought they both seem to be in a jovial mood.

"So -- what did you find out about Jack London -- at our library?" Vern asked, leaning back on the couch.

"That his new house burned down -- just as it was almost finished," Tom said, then sipped his martini.

"Yeah," Vern said, "there's a rumor that the locals set the fire -- because they didn't like London's life-style. He let bums stay on the farm out back -- guys from the road -- just passing through."

"I'd like to see the 'Wolf House,'" Tom said.

"Tomorrow," Vern said, "we can drive up to Sonoma -- for a look-see. I'm taking off two days from the office."

"We're set for the negotiations -- next month -- we have the groundwork done."

"Tomorrow?" Tom said, nodding. "That'll be great."

"And after my class," Bliss said, holding up her martini like a salut, "I'm going to the All People's Church -- so tomorrow, you guys are on your own for dinner."

Tom sat wondering, if Vern knew about the music and dancing at the church after service, and if Bliss told him about the rose kid at the school cafeteria, but he said nothing.

He just nodded, telling himself to keep out of their problems.

Then Tom said, "What about the kids?"

"They will be next door with Missus Kelsey," Bliss said. "Remember, you guys, no later than six o'clock tomorrow. Okay?"

"And for Friday night," Vern said while reaching to pour more martini from the container, "there's a party up at a big beach mansion in Sausalito -- and we're all invited."

"I don't have party clothes," Tom said. "All I got is a white shirt, and my motley sports coat."

"I'll loan you a Hawaiian shirt," Vern said sitting back on the couch. "It's sort of an artsy-craftsy party -- the wife of one of our firm lawyers -- sold a painting she did."

"Is she a good artist?" Tom asked.

"Some friends of theirs -- over in another law firm, bought it -- because it was a large painting -- and they wanted something large to hang in the conference room."

Bliss waived her arm, "You'll like Sausalito, Tom. It's almost like Carmel -- only with big houses in the hills -- and the ocean right outside the door."

"And there's a great restaurant up there," Vern said, "that everybody goes to -- and part of it is open to the sky -- no roof. Before the party -- we'll have dinner there. It's right on the ocean."

They both seem to be getting excited, Tom thought. He was enjoying their enthusiasm; glad they had something to be cheerful about for a change.

"Maybe I shouldn't tag along," he said. "You two could make it a night out together."

"We want to show you California, Tom," Bliss said in an even voice, as if talking to a child.

"You'll get a kick out of it," Vern said. "You'll see how the yuppies live out here."

"I'm getting hungry," he said to Bliss, "what's for dinner, babe?"

"Let's order pizza," she said. "The kids love pizza."

"Hot pizza, and cold beer," Vern said looking at her. "You can't beat that."

*   *   *   *   *

After pizza, Tom and Vern went for a ride in the Porsche, for what Vern said was a "mystery trip."

"You and Kyle been out hustling at the horse track, lately?" Vern asked, as they were driving on the road along the water reservoir that Tom looked at frequently from the house.

Tom knew he was just making conversation, and went along with the talk, growing curious.

"Not too much," he said. "Funny -- but today I called him a couple times -- no one answered the phone."

"Maybe the termites -- got him."

Vern laughed, holding his head back for a moment, then said, "Poor old Kyle -- and those termites. You know, he signed a contract with the State -- that requires over an eighteen month time period, he has to replace all the foundation timbers under that house.

"The State government sold Kyle the house without a down payment -- on the stipulation -- that he replace the timbers the termites have been chewing on."

"It don't look," Tom said, "like he's done <u>any</u> work at all."

"He'll get kicked out of that house -- if he defaults on the contract with the State," Vern said, turning onto a newly paved road. "He knows that."

"He's flat broke," Tom said. "How can he fix up the timbers?"

"There's no basement in that house," Vern said, avoiding Tom's comment. "It sits on posts driven into the hillside -- and the termites have been eating the posts -- and the timbers that support the floor."

"Any day," Vern said smiling, "the <u>whole</u> damn house could slide down the hill onto the road below."

"No kidding?" Tom asked.

"Yeah," Vern said, "that's why the State condemned the place. It's a hazard."

Before Tom could say anything, Vern blurted, "Here we are -- the end of our 'mystery trip.'"

Tom looked over at the sign, Walnut Grove Subdivision, as they drove past. He could see rows of newly built houses ahead with no grass, only bare dirt, and fresh-gray cement driveways and sidewalks, as they drove up the street.

Vern turned the car into a driveway, where an Austin-Healy was parked near the house.

When Tom saw the car, he yelled, "Carl Heminger -- you bastard, Vern!"

"C'mon, kiddo," Vern said, opening the door of the Porsche on his side, "say hello to your old buddy."

"What else can I do?" Tom said, opening the car door on his side of the car. "There's no way I can get out of this --"

"Carl was a big help," Vern said, as they walked up to the brick house, "when Bliss and I were moving out here from Detroit -- hauling all our belongings in a trailer.

"He wanted to come back to California -- he even did most of the driving."

"Okay, okay," Tom said, "but I'm still going to <u>strangle</u> you and Bliss -- for conspiring -- setting me up for this."

Carl came to the front door in Levi's and a t-shirt, and when he saw Vern and Tom, he smiled, swinging open the screen door. Tom realized he was expecting them as company.

"Long time, no see, Tom," Carl said, an uneasy smile on his face, below gold-rimmed eyeglasses, and near bald head.

"Yeah," Tom said shaking hands, "I came out to see what all the excitement in California is about." Smelling the new-house odor, he added, "Nice digs you got here, Carl."

"We think it's grand," his wife said in an English accent, coming out of the kitchen. "Hello, Vern."

"This is my wife, Heather -- Tom Kemp," Carl said weakly.

"Oh, yes," she said, "you're the boyhood friend of Carl's, from Detroit. Nice to meet you."

Tom smiled, looking at her thin, middle-age body, as she shook hands quickly, pulling her hand back.

"Sit down, you guys," Carl said. "We've got Olympia beer -- if that's okay."

"As long as it's cold," Vern said, bumping Tom toward an overstuffed chair.

Tom sat down, looking at Carl going for the beer, noticing he had grown balder since the last time he had seen him. Now, he was practically a duplicate of his father, the buzzard who checked-out Tom's drinking with that phony ride to close the cabin.

Carl sat on the couch opposite Tom, holding his can of beer by the rim, "My sister moved out here to Seattle," Carl said, attempting to make conversation. "She and her plumber husband have four kids now."

"Elspeth, out here?" Tom said smiling. "What next?"

"I've got to finish the dishes," Heather said, and went back to the kitchen. She was uneasy about Tom.

Vern, who had been watching Tom closely, in the event he attempted to confront Carl, said, "We hear you're a new father -- huh, Carl -- now you got to act responsible."

"Come to the back bedroom, you guys," Carl said, getting up from the couch, setting his can of beer on the new hardwood floor.

Tom and Vern followed him into the hallway. Inside the back bedroom, as Carl moved the door open, Tom saw a baby crib, a pink mesh curtain hanging down from the corner of the ceiling, covering the crib. A soft light came from a lamp on a small side table.

"Beautiful," Tom whispered to Carl. "Boy or girl angel?"

"A girl," Heather whispered, standing behind them.

"Come on, everybody," Vern whispered. "Let her sleep."

They all moved down the hallway, Heather closing the door quietly. No one spoke.

In the living room, Tom was finishing his can of beer, when he heard Vern say, "We're going to run, Carl, I've got a bone-crushing day tomorrow -- at the office."

Carl stood nodding, while crossing his hands over his crotch, seemed relieved.

"Good to see you again," Tom said, handing Carl the empty beer can. "You've done all right -- out here in sunny California -- you mug."

Carl smiled patiently, then followed Tom and Vern to the front door. Then, Heather came to the door.

Vern, turned before stepping off the porch, "You folks -- you'll have to visit us in Berkeley -- real soon," he said to them.

"I'll phone Bliss -- next week," Heather said, standing next to Carl, her arms folded.

Driving in the Porsche, Vern said, "That wasn't so bad, huh, Tom -- saying hello to Carl? Bliss thinks it's just being courteous -- she put me up to it."

"That crib," Tom said, "it looked like a shrine."

"It is a shrine in that bedroom," Vern said. "The baby has malformed kidneys. It won't survive to the end of the year."

CHAPTER 15

The day-trip to Sonoma County and the "Wolf House" was cancelled by a phone call the next morning.

Vern explained to Tom, "Someone in our office read the damn State statute wrong -- a state lawyer contends -- so I got to go to the office and meet with my team."

They had been sitting at the kitchen table, having bagels and cream cheese, when Vern answered the wall phone.

Bliss was gone for the day, her class in Oakland, and later, she was going to the All People's Church.

"How long you think you'll be at the office?" Tom said, looking up at Vern from the table.

"I can't say for sure, Tom, but I'll take the kids to Missus Kelsey's house -- until four. If the office session runs later than that, I'll phone Melanie to come over -- and babysit."

"I was just wondering how long it <u>might</u> take," Tom said, "I mean, I could wait -- if it was just going to be an hour or so."

"I wish I knew, kid," Vern said while walking over to a closet. He took out a tan hopsack sports coat, and was pulling it on, while he said, "I've been blindsided by this glitch at the office. I don't know how long it will take to sort out -- so, I guess you're on your own -- sorry -- but duty calls."

"There's plenty I can do," Tom said.

Vern opened his wallet.

"Here's ten bucks," he said handing it to Tom. "Gas money for the Bultaco."

"Na-aw," Tom said.

"Take it, Tom, you've been good for morale around here," he said, setting the bill on the kitchen table.

"I can hang around the house -- write," Tom said, looking at the money. "Maybe read some."

"I'll call here about four," Vern said putting on his Bromide glasses, that change shades with the light, "the same time I phone Melanie to bring the kids home."

"What if I go out?" Tom said, feeling indecisive about what he was going to do. He felt let down; he had wanted to see the "Wolf House," and now he was working to change his mind.

"Well, lock up the house if you go out," Vern said, "and if you're here with Melanie -- behave yourself."

"That sounds like jealousy," Tom said. "The whole thing is up to Melanie."

Grinning and walking to the front door, Vern shook his head.

Tom went over to the wall phone, and was dialing Kyle, when he heard the Porsche start, and roar down the driveway.

When Kyle answered, Tom asked, "Can we go to Sonoma -- on the Bultaco -- and be back by four o'clock?"

"Sure," Kyle said. "But what about money? I'm broke. I was going to pawn something -- go to the horse track."

"I got money," Tom said. "Vern was going to drive me up to Sonoma for a look at the 'Wolf House,' but his office called with an emergency."

"All right," Kyle said. "Pick me up."

When they were filling the tank at a gas station, Kyle said, "Hey -- I <u>might</u> have a job -- selling yachts."

"No kidding," Tom said smiling.

"I met a guy I knew in the army -- at the track -- and he sells yachts. He told me his office lost a salesman," Kyle said, wiping the spilled gas off the motorcycle tank, "and they're looking for a -- replacement.

"He's going to put in a good word for me -- hell, if you can sell encyclopedias, man, you can sell <u>anything</u>."

Kyle started the motorcycle, as Tom stood laughing, then said, "I'll drive -- I know the way to Sonoma."

On the Bultaco behind Kyle, Tom could view the places they drove past, study them, free from watching traffic. What he could not get accustomed to, was the brown leaves and grass, and the warm weather, so close to Halloween.

Passing the Presidio at the San Francisco side of the Golden Gate Bridge, Tom shouted, "What's that building?"

"An old army fort," Kyle shouted. "Built to protect the bay from enemy attack."

When they were crossing on the Golden Gate Bridge, Tom shouted, "Ah-h, the gateway to the vast Pacific!"

"Yeah," Kyle shouted, "and that clump of buildings -- on that island to the right -- with that water tank sticking up -- that's Alcatraz."

"No kidding?" Tom said, tasting the salt air. "Looks grim."

"It's <u>grimmer</u> inside," Kyle shouted above the car traffic noise. "It's closed now. They give tours -- inside."

"No thanks," Tom said.

"Al Capone was a prisoner there," Kyle shouted as they came near the end of the bridge.

Tom was looking at how dry the land was in Sonoma County, when Kyle suddenly turned off the road, and into the parking lot of a winery.

They parked the motorcycle in front of a building with the sign: Visitor Center.

"Let's try the wine," Kyle said, pushing his eyeglasses up higher on his nose. "They give free samples."

"Sounds great," Tom said as they walked to the entrance. "Ah-h," he said, "they put this California sunshine in a bottle."

They each had a glass of Burgundy, poured by the blond girl, who Tom smiled at continually, as she filled glasses from behind the bar, for the line of tourists waiting for a free sample.

When the girl saw there was wine left in the pitcher, she filled Tom's glass a second time, before going to refill it.

He was still smiling at the girl, when he felt the bump of Kyle's forearm.

"Let's get going, Tom. One glass is my limit -- I'm driving."

Tom gulped down the wine, and waiving to the blond girl, followed Kyle outside.

"Some of those tourists," Kyle said, "make a day out of going from winery to winery for the samples."

"Sounds like fun," Tom said watching Kyle upright the Bultaco. Then looking up at the sun, added, "You can almost <u>feel</u> the dry up here -- that's why Sonoma is great for wine grape growing."

"Yeah," Kyle said, "I read that the old missionaries moved the Indians away from the Bay; they were getting sick in the damp San Francisco climate."

"It <u>would</u> be damp down by the Bay," Tom said. "It's right next to the -- open Pacific Ocean."

He flung apart his arms, feeling the effect of the wine.

"The missionaries were from Europe," Kyle said, "they knew how to grow grapes -- in a warm climate like here. It was the beginning of the wine industry -- for the whole of Napa Valley," he said starting the motorcycle.

Tom, climbing on the back of the Bultaco, said, "I wonder how old that girl behind the bar was."

Kyle, smiling, drove out of the parking lot onto a narrow paved road.

"The 'Wolf House' should be right up ahead," Kyle shouted, when they came around a long curve.

Tom looked at the cluster of houses, close by the road, and thought they looked like the old-style cottages back in Michigan. Most of them had screened-in porches and were made with boards that were sagging now.

"There it is," Kyle said, pointing. "That's the 'Wolf House' right over there," he said, stopping the Bultaco at the side of the road.

"Can I walk over there for a closer look?" Tom said, sliding off the back of the motorcycle, standing.

"What for?" Kyle asked. "It's just a pile of rocks -- and charcoal, now."

Tom stood, studying the thick horizontal timbers, charred by the blaze, thinking those must be for the second story of the house, sensing it was a giant house -- a mansion.

Looking along the base of the house, he saw bushes growing around large columns of stones cemented together, the supports for the second story, and he gasped at the size of the house.

It was so well designed, he thought, walking away from Kyle, looking hard, sensing the thought and pleasure London must have had, when planning the house to his wants. It was a work of the heart.

"It caught fire," he said slowly, "just when it was almost completed."

"What did you say?" Kyle said, walking up behind, pushing the motorcycle by the handlebars.

"Nothing," Tom said, licking his lips, tasting the residue of the wine. "London didn't want to -- rebuild -- the house?"

"No," Kyle said. "He overdosed on morphine -- days after the fire." Putting down the kickstand on the Bultaco, he leaned it over on the stand. "That's the cottage -- there -- where he lived while the house was being built. He slept out on the screened porch -- and that's where he took the overdose."

They walked over to the cottage, and Tom peered through the screen, shading his eyes from the bright afternoon sun.

"Poor Jack London," Tom said. "Everything he tried doing in life -- it seems there was a conspiracy against him -- to make <u>sure</u> he failed."

"What?" Kyle said. "I didn't hear you."

"He was just a kid from the wrong side of the tracks," Tom said, straightening up from looking through the screen. "London's past caught up with him -- when he made some headway."

"He was involved in the Socialist movement," Kyle said. "And a lot of people didn't like him for that."

"Maybe all that was the reason he overdosed," Tom said.

"Oh," Kyle said, "he had some kind of kidney disease -- that bloated him -- made him look like a sausage. He was really sick when he overdosed."

"Sick at heart," Tom mumbled.

"What?" Kyle asked, pushing up his eyeglasses.

"Thanks for showing me 'Wolf House,' man," Tom said. "I'm learning a lot -- from the places you've shown me out here in California."

Walking back to the motorcycle, Kyle said, "You know -- a lot of people with troubles -- back East -- they come running West, out here to California -- and this is as far as they can go -- because of the Pacific Ocean. Some jump off the Golden Gate Bridge into the ocean -- they can't run any further."

"Well," Tom said, climbing on the back of the Bultaco, behind Kyle, the engine running, "maybe the trick is -- to avoid trouble."

"Yeah," Kyle said, looking forward, "that would work."

Tom took a quick glance at the "Wolf House," thinking Jack London built himself an oversize cabin, giant rooms, stone fireplace, and even a second floor. But someone took it away -- burned it.

If they shot him, it would have had the same result.

*   *   *   *   *

Vern was home at five-thirty, later that afternoon; Tom saw the Porsche, when he drove the Bultaco up the hill to the house, after dropping off Kyle at his girlfriend's apartment.

When Tom walked into the house, he saw the children, home from Missus Kelsey's next door, and Vern, eating dinner at the kitchen table.

"What you eating?" Tom said to Shelly, walking up behind her.

"Swedish meatballs," she said, holding one up on the end of her fork. "He's eating gravy," she said, pointing to Frederick in his high chair, who was eating with a spoon, mashed potatoes, flooded with gravy, a single meatball in the center of the plate.

"You must have found Kyle," Vern said from the table.

"Yeah," Tom said, "we rode the Bultaco up to Sonoma. I got to see the house that Jack built -- that somebody torched."

Vern nodded, smiling up at him.

"Have some meatballs," he said. "Bliss made a pile of them," and Tom saw him glance at Bliss's chair.

"Thanks," Tom said, while sitting down.

He took two slices of bread, and made a sandwich with three meatballs.

Shelly, watching him, took a slice of bread and made a small sandwich with one meatball.

Tom grinned at her.

"Want something to drink?" Vern asked him; Tom seeing he was drinking martinis, but not offering one.

"I need a beer," Tom said. "I'm dried out from that windy motorcycle ride. All I've had to drink all day -- was a double Burgundy wine sample -- with the rest of the free loaders at the winery up at Sonoma."

"There should be a few cans in the fridge," Vern said, and again, Tom saw him look at the chair that Bliss sat on.

As Tom stood opening the beer, he looked at Vern, distracted, and knew he was regretting letting Bliss go to that blowout party at that church. Maybe he was wondering too, Tom thought, if there would be marijuana smoke in the air.

Tom, silent, sat back down at the table and picked up the meatball sandwich.

"You think they'll be smoking pot -- at that party?" Vern asked slowly.

"They probably don't allow drinking," Tom said, and took a bite of the sandwich. Then talking with his mouth full, added, "Somebody always has a joint."

"I know Bliss takes a toke -- now and then," Vern said looking at Frederick, who was now eating mashed potatoes with his hand.

"Maybe so" Tom said, holding his sandwich in front of his face with both hands, thinking hard of something to say, to ease Vern's mind, "but -- girls -- like dancing, when there's music -- and they don't have much time for smoking."

Vern reached over with a napkin to wipe the side of the baby's face; there were mashed potatoes and gravy almost to Frederick's ear.

"She <u>deserves</u> a night out," he said, sitting back, picking up his martini glass. "She's been cooped-up here with the kids -- too long.

"I'm away too much," he said, taking a sip from his glass. "But I <u>got</u> to make the money."

He was trying to convince himself that Bliss being out for the night, was nothing to be apprehensive about. Tom understood, and said, "She won't be out long -- a few hours more - -she'll be home."

"I'm just used to having her home," Vern said, "when I'm home -- that's all."

"Yeah," Tom said, and bit into his sandwich.

Later, Tom watching the news on television, the children playing on the floor with a robot truck that had an electronic device that guided its movement, that they continually ran into the wall, scattering its load of plastic toys, making them laugh, asked, "Who's this girl on TV? The announcer dame -- she looks familiar -- sort of."

He was sitting on the couch, drinking another beer, the children on the floor in front of him.

Vern was in the kitchen, stacking the dishes in the dishwasher, and he came out to look at the screen.

"That's Pia Lindstrom," he said. "She's Ingrid Bergman's daughter -- from the first marriage -- to that doctor -- Peter Lindstrom."

"She doesn't look much like her movie-star mother," Tom said.

He had been wanting a smoke, and when he saw the open pack of Benson-Hedges cigarettes on the table in front of the couch, he reached for one. He felt the English cigarettes were out of place, somehow.

"Pia's still a winner," Vern said, standing in front of the television set.

The front door opened, and Bliss came in, saying "I can't put the big car in the garage -- the Porsche is in the way."

"I'll put the car in the garage," Tom said getting up.

Standing in front of Bliss, his hand out, he looked at her eyes. They were dilated. She was high.

"Give me the keys," he said to her, grinning, and she grinned back, for his knowing she had been smoking pot.

"Go easy," he whispered. "He's been worrying about you," he said as she bent down to pick up the baby.

Vern snapped off the television set, asking Bliss, "Was that church -- all you expected it to be?"

Tom heard him ask her, as he was walking to the front door, scooping the Porsche keys off the table in the foyer, hoping that he would not discover she was swacked.

When he came back into the house, they were sitting on the couch, and Tom heard Vern say, "It's okay, if you didn't sign anything."

"That church is a racket. They work to get pledges -- money from the suburbs."

"No, I didn't sign anything," Bliss said, reaching for the English cigarettes, then lighting one. "Most of the time, me and my friends -- were practicing dance steps. They were teaching me to do slide dancing.

"The music was just fabulous -- the whole party was fabulous."

"Were there any -- whites -- there?" Vern asked quietly.

"Oh -- yes," Bliss said, blowing smoke out, watching Tom walking over to stand in front of the low table, "they were mostly girls."

Vern looking up, asked Tom, "You going to stay in -- tonight?"

"Yeah," he said, "I got a lot of notes to put in my journal. Then later -- I want to phone Ann."

The cigarette Bliss was smoking, slipped from her fingers and fell on the rug in front of her. She was unaware it fell.

Vern did not see it drop; he suddenly looked over at the children, when the yellow truck struck a tall glass vase holding a fern plant, and nearly fell over.

Tom picked up the cigarette, quickly, and began smoking it.

"That's enough for tonight," Bliss said to the children, and when she saw Tom, smoking, she smiled up at him, knowing he had picked it up, and shrugged.

"I gave you ten extra minutes to play," she said to the children, getting up from the couch, "and now it's time for your bath."

Vern getting up also, taking hold of the martini shaker, said to Tom, "I'll mix another batch of martinis for a nightcap -- stay here, sluggo."

"Hey," Bliss said to Vern as he stepped over to the liquor cabinet, "can't you guys take it easy on the drinking? You know we have a heavy schedule tomorrow.

"You can drink at the party tomorrow night."

"We'll just have one," Vern said without looking at her.

Tom stood watching Bliss as she bent down to pick up the baby from the floor, her dress pulling tight on her bottom.

"The leaves are covering the patio," Bliss said from the entrance to the hallway, to Vern, who stood mixing the martinis at the liquor cabinet. "We don't want a fire out there," she said, shifting the weight of the baby in her arms. "Do we?"

"Okay," he said, turning away from the cabinet, and Tom saw him roll his eyes up, "I'll rake the patio tomorrow."

Tom could see the confrontation coming, and he did not want to hear it. Bliss's involvement with the party church was over; Tom could see Vern's drinking was just to bolster himself to telling her so.

To get away, Tom said, "Maybe I should call Detroit now, see what Ann's doing. Can I use the phone in your office?" he said as Vern came back to the couch.

"Use the one in the kitchen," he said setting the martini shaker on the low table, "I've got all my paperwork and notes spread out on the desk."

"Right," Tom said, nodding.

CHAPTER 16

Ann Calthorp's father answered the phone when Tom called Detroit.

"She went up to Birmingham," he said in his detached way of speaking, as if he was thinking of something else, "ah, with some of her painter friends. Some kind of art showing -- I think she said."

"Okay, Mister Calthorp," Tom said, louder than usual for the old man to hear, "will you tell her I phoned? Please."

"Yes -- yes, I'll tell her."

Tom hung up the wall phone, reaching from the chair at the kitchen table where he was sitting, then shook his head.

"Damn," he said softly, "I guess I can't expect her to sit at home -- waiting."

When Tom walked out to the sitting room, Vern was not sitting on the couch, but the martini shaker was on the low table where he left it.

When he saw the light on in Vern's study, he walked over to the doorway.

"You want to skip the nightcap martini?" Tom said from the doorway, expecting him to agree; he was reading intently.

"No, no-o," he said getting up from his desk, snapping off the desk light. "Never skip a nightcap -- it's bad for your -- nerves."

Tom was suspicious about him now, wondering what he was going to do about Bliss's church, why he could suddenly engross himself in his legal work, then act, now, as if he had something else, important, on his mind.

He was going in too many directions all at once. Tom could not follow, but he thought he would wait.

Back in the kitchen, Vern was pouring martinis from the shaker he carried in, while he asked Tom, "Have you -- given any thought -- to <u>moving</u> out here to California?"

Why Vern wanted to sit in the kitchen, Tom could not understand.

There it is, Tom thought, he's getting anxious about me hanging around the house. I'm going to hear my being a guest is coming to a close, he told himself.

"This tourist bit is terrific," Tom said, avoiding Vern's question about moving to California, "but what I'd like -- is to meet people like Steinbeck -- who live in their father's garage -- doing their work -- writing -- or whatever."

"Ah-h," Vern said, lifting his martini from the table, "that's the artsy-craftsy crowd -- they hang out in the town of Venice -- on the coast -- I hear, kid."

91

"Maybe I'll do some scouting over there," Tom said, then looking at the wall telephone, said, "I called Ann -- she's out with friends. I hope she has not given up on me -- and my wandering around."

Tom was saying anything he could think of, just to keep talking, hoping Vern would say what was bothering his mind.

Tom was sipping his martini, when Vern said calmly, "Women are -- possessive. That -- can be a problem -- sometimes."

Bliss came through the kitchen door, wearing a bathrobe, the kids with her, "What kind of a problem?" she asked, shifting the baby in her arms, turning to look at Shelly back in the doorway.

"We were talking about -- Tom's girl -- back in Detroit," Vern said lying, looking at Tom, as if to say to him, 'keep quiet, please,' "and about her not being home -- when he phoned just now."

"What do you expect, Tom?" Bliss said, looking at the baby in her arms, dressed in a tiger-striped costume with ears and a tail. Then she said, "We've been trying on our costumes for Missus Kelsey's Halloween party tomorrow -- at lunchtime. It's for all the little ones she babysits."

"I'm a fairy princess," Shelly said from the doorway, waiving her wand, turning around to show her tiara and short pink shirt.

"You'll be the belle of the ball, honey," Vern said to her.

"I hope you don't turn into a pumpkin," Tom said to her, grinning, teasing.

The phone rang, and Vern stood up and stepped by Shelly in the doorway, saying, "Now what?" He went to his office.

Bliss had taken chocolate pudding cups out of the fridge for the children, and they were eating at the table, when she tapped Tom's wrist with a spoon.

He smiled at her, nodding, knowing she was saying, 'I have to get out once in a while -- for a change -- marijuana and all.'

Vern came back, his face drawn, and sat down at the table.

"That's odd," he said picking up his martini glass, "I was sure we had the pre-negotiation plans all set."

"You look worried Vern," Bliss said. "Is it serious?"

"I have to go to the office in San Francisco, on Saturday morning yet -- for what -- I don't understand.

"My secretary says, two guys are coming from Washington, D.C. to discuss --new Federal Labor Law changes. That's crazy.

"The two guys are tied up until Saturday -- so that's when they're coming -- for some reason."

"Well," Bliss said, picking up the baby Frederick out of his high chair, wiping his face, "maybe you want to call off going to Sausalito tomorrow, honey?"

"No, no," Vern said, smiling weakly. "I just won't be able to get too drunk," he said sitting back in his chair.

"If that's what you want," Bliss said to Vern. Then reaching for Shelly's hand, added, "We're off to bed. Don't be too long down here, you two -- tomorrow's another day."

"We'll take a bit longer," Vern said, taking a sip of his martini, watching the children and Bliss go out, then shouting, "I'll be upstairs in twenty minutes."

Tom, feeling the gin, wanted to say something positive, so he said, "I'm thinking of asking Kyle -- to find me a cheap apartment -- somewhere near his art school -- for me to locate for a book-length stay.

"I'd like to hang out here in California -- a while longer."

"Hey, that's great," Vern said, sipping what was left of his martini, "glad to hear you dig it out here."

He spoke, but Tom could see his mind was still centered on the trouble at his office.

"I've been writing a lot of notes in my journal," Tom said, just to keep the conversation going, "and it's building toward a book-size story."

"Now -- all I need is to find permanent digs -- a place I can do some writing."

Vern was pouring more martinis into Tom's glass, when he said, "You can stay here with us, kid -- as long as you need to.

"There's no problem -- you were invited out here to test the water -- no matter how long it takes, doesn't matter."

"Thanks, man," Tom said, then after sipping his drink, watching Vern drink his, added, "I'll try to stay out of the way -- of the day-to-day routine."

"Don't worry about that," Vern said, finishing his drink. "There's so much going on -- around this house -- that you'll just be another -- another bump in the road."

Tom looked at him, wondering what he meant.

*   *   *   *   *

Friday morning, Tom walked into the kitchen and saw Vern drinking coffee. He was alone at the table.

"Bliss and the kids just left," he said. "Missus Kelsey phoned and asked for help setting up the Halloween party stuff -- so they went over early -- the kids in their costumes already."

Tom was pouring coffee into a cup, when Vern asked, "What you got on tap for today?"

"If I can find Kyle," Tom said, sitting down at the table, across from Vern, "I'd like to go to the horses -- pick up a few bucks at the track."

"I've got a guitar lesson at eleven with my instructor, but after that," Vern said grimacing, "I've got to do some yard work around the house."

"You want some help raking?"

"Naw," Vern said, "it takes about a half hour -- and I need the exercise. You want a shot in your coffee -- you look like you could use one?"

"It's too early," Tom said rubbing the stubble on his chin. "I'll wait to do the drinking at the party tonight in Sausalito."

The wall telephone rang, and Vern reached from his chair to answer it.

"Kyle," he said, "how's it going?" There was a pause, then he added, "Yeah, he's here -- we're just having coffee."

Tom took the phone, the cable-coil stretching across the table, saying, "I've been looking for you -- I phoned."

"I need your help," Kyle said, softly. "I didn't make it home last night -- you got to help me snow my wife -- so I can get back in the house. Will you come and get me?"

"Where are you now?" Tom asked grinning.

"Laura's apartment -- you know, across from the Art School." There was a pause, "Hey, have you shaved yet?"

"No. Why?"

"Good," Kyle said, his voice turning hopeful, "you'll look more like you've been up all night. And wear the same shirt -- you wore yesterday. Okay?"

"So you spent the night at Laura's?" Tom said, half kidding Kyle.

Vern, who had been listening, began laughing as he stood up to get more coffee.

"I'll fill you in on all that," Kyle said quietly, sounding desperate again, "when you get here with the Bultaco. Okay?" There was a silent moment. Then whispering, he said, "Laura loaned me five bucks -- I'll give you half for gas."

"All right," Tom said, "I'll be there as soon as I can."

Handing the phone back across the table to Vern, Tom said, "He's been over at his girlfriend's all night -- he needs my help to con Doris -- so he can get back in the house."

"Ah-h," Vern said hanging up the phone, "'what a curious web we weave -- when we set out to deceive', or something like that."

"He's really sweating it out," Tom said, getting up from the table, gulping some coffee. "I better get on my horse -- get over there."

"You need a few bucks, Tom?"

"Naw -- it's more fun -- when the money's short," he said lying.

When Tom drove up to the apartment house on the motorcycle, he saw Kyle sitting outside on the steps.

His clothes were rumpled.

"You look like something the cat dragged in," Tom said. "Get on."

"No," Kyle said, wiping the dust off the back of his pants, as he got to his feet, 'I'm starving -- there's a bakery down the block here -- you can get a day-old Danish for a quarter. We'll go there -- and I can tell you my plan for getting back in the house."

Kyle watched as Tom lowered the kickstand, and leaned the Bultaco over, saying, "Sometimes -- there's an apricot Danish in the pile -- on the bakery counter."

Tom could not stop smiling, as he walked with Kyle up the block to the bakery. He wondered how Kyle could think of pastry, when he had a dilemma facing him at home.

"I've been reading up on boats," Kyle said, opening the door of the bakery. "I'm learning what is a mizzen-mast, thwarts, gunnels, and even a Genoa jib -- all that stuff, in case I land that new job -- selling yachts."

"That's a good idea, Kyle."

Tom watched as Kyle picked out two Blueberry Danish from the pile on a tray, sitting on the counter, then asked the old lady behind the counter for two cups of coffee.

"No apricot today," he said leading Tom to a small table near the window, where they sat down on old-style wire chairs.

"You can't be a winner everyday," Tom said, turning to look out the window at the traffic to hide his grinning.

The coffee in the paper cup was so hot, Tom had to hold it with his thumb on the rim, a finger on the bottom.

"I was sure a winner last night," Kyle said, and bit into the Danish. "Laura is auditioning for a part in "HAIR" -- you know, the musical."

Tom nodded, blowing on the hot coffee.

"Her audition is set for Monday -- and she wanted me to help her learn the lines -- and to get her used to being -- bare-breasted -- for the part."

"Terrific," Tom said juggling the coffee.

"We were drinking some wine," Kyle said. "And pretty soon <u>all</u> Laura's clothes were off," he said, pointing at the second Danish, and when Tom nodded, he picked it up.

"We both got excited," Kyle said chewing, "and by the time we made it -- three times -- it was getting late. She was going to drive me home -- but I wanted her more than anything. I couldn't help it. I couldn't stop -- there are some women like that -- you just want to be with them."

"Yeah," Tom said, sipping the coffee, "time flies -- you have to watch time -- especially when you're having fun."

Kyle, chewing and nodding, said, "I know better -- than to stay out all night."

"So what are you going to do now, Kyle?"

"I'm going to tell Doris we went to Reno on the Bultaco -- we were on the road all night."

"You think that will float with her?"

"She trusts me."

Later, when they drove up to Kyle's house on the motorcycle, his wife was unloading groceries from the Volkswagen.

"You two look like you just got out of jail," she said, holding a full shopping bag on each side of her pregnant stomach.

"We've been on the road all night," Kyle said, getting off the back of the Bultaco. "Tom wanted to see Reno -- after we got to Lake Tahoe."

Tom sat listening amazed how convincing Kyle sounded.

"Didn't you sleep -- at all?" Doris asked, starting up the steps to the door of the house.

"We tried," Kyle said, moving around her to pull open the screen door, "but it was too cold in the mountains -- we stretched out on picnic benches in a roadside park -- but gave up."

"You're lucky," Doris said going into the house, "that the police didn't grab you."

Holding the door open, Kyle turned to Tom, rolling up his eyes, lifting his glasses at the same time, as if to say, 'I'm off the hook.'

When Doris came back to the door, Tom standing astride over the motorcycle, said, "It was all my fault -- Kyle was out all night. I asked him to show me Jack London's 'Wolf House' up in Sonoma -- that's how the whole trip -- started."

For some reason, he felt he was only telling a half-truth, not a complete lie, as Doris acted as if she did not hear him.

As she was passing Kyle at the doorway, starting down the steps, said to him, "Don't you have an art class today?"

"I'm too tired," he said following her down to the car. "I would have stayed home -- after that ride -- if I <u>was</u> here this morning. I got saddle-sores."

"Serves you right," she said to him at the car, handing him a dozen grapefruit in a mesh bag. "You should know better."

Tom, having heard enough, turned the handlebars of the Bultaco, after starting it, headed downhill, shouting, "Kyle -- call me Sunday -- we'll watch football."

"You going?" Doris shouted. "Don't you want coffee?"

"I got to sleep," Tom shouted. "The Hurley's are taking me to a party tonight -- a bunch of lawyers in Sausalito."

"I'll phone you Sunday," Kyle shouted. "About eleven," he added, twirling the bag of grapefruit.

*   *   *   *   *

Driving on the road to the Hurley house, passing where Melanie lived, Tom spotted a Karmann Ghia with heavy rusting above the left front wheel, parked at an odd angle off the road, almost in the bushes.

When he caught a glimpse of Melanie's face, he drove up to the side of the car and stopped.

"You need help?" he said looking at her. "Car break down?"

The young man next to her, when he straightened up, Tom saw he wore a white shirt and a black tie.

Then Tom spotted the small brown paper bag he was holding, the handle of a pistol showing.

"What you two doing?" he said, immediately thinking of Bonnie and Clyde.

"He's all right," Melanie said to the young man, who up close, Tom could see was trying to grow a mustache. "Jarred is just showing me how to -- take the bullets out of my mother's gun," she said, looking up at Tom.

"When she falls asleep, I want to sneak it from under the couch -- where she hides it," Melanie said leaning forward, "and I want to take the bullets out -- and put it back."

Tom, who was getting excited by her pleading look, her blond hair falling to partially cover her face, said, "But whose gun is in the paper bag?"

"It's my dad's," Jarred said. "He keeps it in the drawer at our pharmacy. It's the same kind Melanie's mother has -- I'm just showing her how to unload it."

Tom smiled, leaning back on the Bultaco seat, "and what are you going to do with the bullets -- from your mother's gun?" he asked to be funny.

"Throw them in the trash," Melanie said, brushing her hair back from her face. "It's Halloween night, Monday, and mother might get upset -- if something <u>unusual</u> happens near the house."

Smiling with relief, Tom said. "Okay, you two -- but remember what happened to Bonnie and Clyde," before he sped away.

Then as he drove, shifting gears on the motorcycle, "I didn't have to say that -- it doesn't even make sense."

What made sense, he told himself, was seeing Melanie with another guy, and not liking it.

CHAPTER 17

Vern was in his study going over his legal papers, when Tom came into the house.

"I can't find <u>anything</u> that needs thrashing over," Vern said, when he saw Tom in the doorway. "For the life of me, man, I can't find what those Washington guys are going to nit-pic tomorrow."

Tom did not want to hear any more about the legal trouble, and he said, "Just let it rest, slick. This time tomorrow -- you'll know all about it."

"You're right, Tom," Vern said, and dropped the folder down on his desk. "To hell with it. It's not worth having a coronary over."

Then, turning off the desk lamp, he said, "Let's have a drink."

Tom, following him to the kitchen, said, "No martinis -- they're too potent."

"How'd Kyle make out -- he get back in the house?" Vern asked, pulling open the refrigerator door.

"He's as click as a green onion," Tom said smiling. "Doris <u>trusts</u> him -- he got back home without a hitch."

"Hey," Vern said, "there's papaya juice in here -- we can have that with some vodka -- a regular health drink."

"I hope Bliss wasn't planning to use it for something," Tom said.

"Naw, we're safe," Vern said taking the bottle out, "anyhow we're going out for dinner tonight."

They had sat down at the table with their drinks, when Bliss came in with the children, the baby sleeping against her shoulder. Shelly was following, carrying two baskets.

"Ah," Vern said to them, "our trick-or-treaters are home."

"They're worn out," Bliss said. "They were excited -- seeing all the other kids in their costumes. They had a ball."

"What's in the baskets?" Vern asked Shelly.

"Candy apples," she said, holding them up. "Missus Kelsey gave us what was left over. And TWIX bars too."

"Good haul," Tom said. "Better make sure you brush your teeth -- after you eat all that stuff."

"I'm going to put them on the bed," Bliss said. "They need to nap -- I do too. I'm pooped." Putting her hand on Shelly's head, she said, "c'mon dear."

She stopped at the hallway, and turned, saying, "Melanie will be here at four o'clock. I made sloppy Joes for the kids, so don't drink <u>all</u> the papaya juice.

"I'll feed them before we go."

"Okay, babe," Vern said to her, nodding. When he turned to Tom he said, "I'm glad to hear -- you're going to locate out here in California -- there's everything out here for a writer."

Tom sensing he was making conversation, while still thinking of his legal trouble, said, "Yeah, the Bay area lives up to all I've heard about it."

Tom did not want to appear too evasive to a lawyer, who can cross examine, so he said, "But there are a lot of loose ends I left back in Detroit -- that I should go back and settle."

"Wait until you see the foxes at the party tonight," Vern whispered across the table. "Tennis-hard women -- lean -- you know what I mean."

Tom, lifting his drink, said, "Hey, you're getting me excited," and took a sip.

"They're all winners, man."

"California golden girls," Tom said being facetious. "Tan and tawny. I can hardly wait to get to this party." He felt relieved now of being cross-examined about moving.

"What time is it?" Vern asked putting down his glass.

"Almost three."

"I still have time to look at my draft of that contract," he said getting to his feet. "I just want to look at it once more," then finished his drink.

"Maybe you could dig out that Hawaiian shirt, you want me to wear tonight," Tom said, getting up from the table.

"In a few minutes, ace," Vern said. "Take a shower. I'll throw the shirt on your bed. It's yellow with pineapples on it. I bought it in Honolulu -- but I don't have the guts to wear it."

"It don't glow in the dark," Tom said, finishing his drink, "or anything like that?"

"I'm not sure," Vern said, as he was walking to his study.

Later, after showering, Tom put on the pineapple shirt, and when he walked out to the sitting room, he saw Melanie.

"How did the unloading go?"

"Perfect," she said, smiling up at him, from watching television. "It all worked out -- like I said."

Vern and Bliss came up behind Tom.

"We better get going," Vern said. "It's sort of a long drive."

Bliss nudged Tom's arm, when she saw he was looking too long at Melanie, wearing a dark blue sweater and skirt.

"See you," Tom said to Melanie. "I'll walk you home."

"You look like a hustler in that shirt," Vern said as they were walking to the big car. "You're bound to be the life of the party."

Bliss, getting into the car, said, "He looks like a fruit juice salesman."

They all laughed.

Sitting in the front seat of the car, next to Bliss, Tom could feel her round, soft thigh, against his.

Crossing on the Golden Gate Bridge, Tom said, "That's Alcatraz over there -- I saw it when Kyle and I crossed here on the Bultaco."

"Yeah," Vern said, as if not wanting to be outdone, "and just behind it -- is Mare Island -- that's where the old China Clipper started from -- for Midway Island and all that.

"But it's closed now -- no more Pan American Airlines. The Navy took over Mare Island now."

"Maybe," Bliss said, "not enough people wanted to go to China."

"Or maybe," Tom said, "World War II had something to do with it."

When he turned from looking at the Bay, to looking out at the Pacific Ocean, flat, the orange sun above the horizon, he had a strange feeling -- that he <u>belonged</u> here.

When they drove up to the restaurant, and Tom saw the valet parking, and all the sports cars in the parking lot, he said to Bliss, "Looks like a swanky place."

Inside the wood paneled dining room, Tom saw one wall opened out to the ocean, like a theatre. Most of the tables, out in the open, were taken by groups of young people, dressed in bright striped or Hawaiian shirts, all of whom, seemed to be laughing or talking loud.

Passing a sign on a stand in the dining room, Tom made a tight face, as he read it.

TONIGHT
BEEF MEDALLIONS -- $35.00
ARTICHOKES ALA CARTE

"I could live two weeks on thirty-five bucks," he said, quietly to Bliss ahead of him.

"Don't worry," she said. "Vern puts it all on his expense account."

Vern lead the way, he followed the hostess carrying an armful of giant menus, who pointed to a table at the edge of where the ceiling ended, opening to the outdoor part of the dining room.

Tom saw Vern slip a folded five-dollar bill into the hostess's hand, holding the menus, as she stood smiling.

Sitting at the table, Tom looked for the least expensive item on the menu, and found:

BAKED SALMON WITH POTATOE WEDGES
$12.95

Vern ordered salad and the medallions, and Bliss ordered the same, but when he ordered martinis, she said, "No -- I want a Mai-Tai."

"What's a Mai-Tai?" Tom asked, after ordering salmon.

"It's a blockbuster drink with five kinds of booze mixed in," Vern said, looking at Bliss. "I think it's a little too strong -- for you, babe."

"If I can't drink it, Tom will. Won't you?"

"Sure," he said. "I'll have a Mai-Tai too," he said to the waitress.

After dinner, Tom was dizzy from the potent drink, having to down most of Bliss's Mai-Tai in addition to his, and when they parked in the driveway of the large hillside manor-house, he said, "Wow -- am I gassed."

"C'mon," Bliss said, "so is everybody else at <u>this</u> party," helping him out of the car, her breasts pressing against his arm.

"Hey," Vern said coming around the big car, "that's an Alfa-Romero over there -- that white convertible, man," and Tom smiled, knowing he had too many martinis. "Beautiful car, man."

Passing the shrubbery that grew right up to the front door of the house, they all walked through the open front door, and Tom stumbled, stepping down the two steps from the foyer that lead to the main room, but Vern caught him by the arm.

Tom, looking up, wondering if anyone saw him stumble, noticed that the people were all absorbed in their conversations, all holding drinks, calmly.

He smiled, relieved, thinking the ceiling could collapse and they would hardly notice.

Most of the men wore Hawaiian shirts, like his, Tom could see, and some of the women wore slacks, informal, but there were some women in skirts, and a single strand of pearls, who looked like they were attending an embassy conclave.

"Hello Vern Hurley," a small woman in a red see-through blouse covering her black bra, said loudly. "I'm Maggie -- Barlow Thompson's wife."

Tom looked at her drink, after studying her blouse, and saw it was a tall pilsner glass of Champagne, and smiled.

"We brought our house guest -- Tom Kemp from Detroit," Vern said studying her blouse, furtively, "and he's feeling his Mai-Tais from dinner. He writes fiction stories."

"Ah-h a writer," Maggie said, "a fellow artist. And what brings you to California -- Mister Kemp?"

"Mai-Tais," Tom said, grinning. "I came to research Mai-Tais. I had one and part of someone else's - and I'm becoming an expert."

Avoiding Tom's comment, Maggie looked up at Vern, saying, "Some people think my painting -- is reminiscent of Paul Klee's work."

Bliss smiled at her, watching her take hold of Vern's arm, "Come meet Barlow," she said, "he claims you're a legal wizard, you know. He'll be glad to see you."

Tom whispered hoarsely to Bliss, "I'd like to go and sleep in the back of the car."

"Maggie," Vern said, looking at Bliss for a moment, tilting his head, asking her approval, "congratulations on selling your painting."

Maggie leaned toward Vern, "I wanted two thousand for it -- but I settled for twelve-hundred."

As Vern nodded, he said, "Tom, why don't you sit down for a while. There's a chair over by the window."

"C'mon, Tom," Bliss said taking his arm, "I'll walk you over to the chair."

Vern took the other arm, and they lead Tom to the chair, and when he sat down, he said, "Why does the room keep moving?"

Barlow Thompson came over to the group around Tom.

"Vern, good to see you again. Hello, Bliss," he said.

Grinning up at Barlow, Tom said, "I'm from Detroit -- I'm a house guest -- I'm Tom Kemp -- your mustache makes you look like Clark Gable."

"Yes, welcome," Barlow said looking at Maggie, contemptuously. Pulling Vern away by the arm, "I got somebody you should meet," he said. "Maybe our next congressman."

"Tom, sit here until you feel better," Bliss said quietly, watching as Maggie moved away to talk with other guests.

"Okay," Tom said, "I'll hold the fort."

He was going to ask Bliss if he could kiss her.

"Hello, Bliss," a thin woman in a swirl of blond hair said; she had appeared out of nowhere. "I haven't seen you -- since your second child. Have you thought of modeling again?"

"La-dee-da," Tom said looking at her. "You should be in the movies."

Bliss took hold of the woman's arm, and without speaking, they walked away from Tom.

Tom sat for a while, elbows on his knees, studying the crowd of people, whom all, it seemed to him, were speaking in low, subdued tones, as if talking of something confidential.

Then he caught a glimpse of a red haired woman, alone, standing at the bar, looking at him.

Then she turned away, after she realized he saw her watching him. He began a sweep, of looking for something interesting happening in the group, and when his glance fell on her again, he caught her looking at him a <u>second</u> time.

He stood up, and slowly walked over to the bar. Standing next to her, he saw she was perfectly groomed, not a hair out of place. She smiled, showing her teeth, and he noticed they were perfect also.

"Could I have a rum and coke, please," he said to her.

"I'm a guest," she said, smiling wider.

"Well, maybe you can help me."

"How?"

"I'm looking for the ocean."

"It's just outside that door."

"Would you show me?" he said. "I've had too many Mai-Tais, and I feel out of place here, with all these successful people."

"Maybe the smell of the sea -- will bring back my confidence."

"All right," she said smiling. "Come along."

Outside on the dark porch, Tom looked up at the sky. "The stars, ah-h, now I can get oriented," he said, moving to sit on the low wall. "I'll be back to myself in no time.

"Did you study the stars in college?" he asked her. "I learned everything I know about stars in college."

"No. I was an economics major at Stanford," she said.

"Well," Tom said, grinning, "no one's perfect."

She smiled, holding her drink up near her face.

"You're Tom Kemp from Detroit," she said. "I heard you say it to Barlow."

"And I was a student for two years -- at Wayne State -- which is not like Stanford. I studied Journalism at Wayne, a lunch-bucket college, where everybody works all day -- and takes night classes - to get ahead in life."

"And now you are writing fiction, I hear," she said.

"I had to turn to fiction -- nobody believes what I say."

She laughed, and said, "Now you're being silly."

"I thought you were a lawyer," Tom said, pulling her closer, sliding his hand down her back to her rump. "If you're not a lawyer -- what do you do?"

"I work in an accounting office."

"And under that dress," he whispered, "you have enough armor to stop a tank battalion. You're like an old lady, who wears a corset -- who packs-in all her sagging parts."

"You're very astute," she whispered back.

"Well groomed," Tom said, "and wearing a corset for protection -- that means you're either military -- or the police.

"You probably even have a clothing allowance."

"You're very observant," she said, backing away slightly.

He took the drink from her hand, saying, "Hey, you're not going to arrest me. -- Are you?"

"You -- shouldn't be living with the Hurleys."

"Ah-h, you're going to arrest me for vagrancy -- and no visible means of support," he said. "Where are your handcuffs?" he said, and sipped her drink.

"We should go back inside," she said. "You seem to be better -- those Mai-Tais are wearing off."
She turned away, and quickly went into the house.

The red haired girl was not in the room, when Tom stepped back into the party, and standing in the door, over to his right, he saw a group of smiling people, watching Bliss doing a slide-dance on a patch of bare floor.

Vern came up, "You okay, Sluggo?"

"I forgot to tell that red head," Tom said, "that Jack London was arrested -- for vagrancy, once. I think it was in Erie, Pennsylvania.

"Oh well, she'll be sorry she ran off -- when I'm rich and famous."

"Don't drink any more, Tom. I work with these people every day -- I don't want any trouble with them. Nothing embarrassing.

"You understand -- I'm in a bind here."

"Hey, Vern -- that red head was a cop -- maybe a Fed. I wonder what they're after me for? Hell, everybody cheats on their Income Tax," Tom said quietly.

"We'll be going in a while," Vern said, glancing at Bliss dancing the step she learned from her friends at the school. His face grew taunt, Tom saw, when he said, "Don't drink anymore -- sit down for a while."

Tom sat down, seeing Bliss frown, when Vern walked over and took hold of her arm, stopping her dance.

Several of the guests clapped, smiling at her performance, while Vern lead her back to where Tom was sitting.

"Why don't you and Bliss go for the car, Tom," he said, still holding Bliss's arm.

He spoke in a tone that was not suggestive, but more like a command.

"Bring it around to the front door," he said, letting go of Bliss's arm.

"I'll say good night for all of us," he said quietly, "try to smooth things over -- for this display."

"Were we that bad?" Tom asked looking at Bliss.

"I don't know why you have to apologize," Bliss said. "Half these guests are blasted -- they love a good time.

"Hell," she said waiving her arm, "they were enjoying my dancing."

"Please -- go get the Mercedes," Vern said in a low, husky voice. "Give me a break -- you two."

"Okay, okay," Tom said. "Give me the keys."

"They're in the ignition," Vern said. "Just bring the car to the door -- I'll drive home."

"C'mon Bliss," Tom said getting up, taking her by the arm, "I guess we're in the doghouse -- the least we can do -- is bring the car up."

"I was just getting my groove," she said, as she and Tom walked toward the front door.

It took them several minutes to locate the Mercedes in the jumble of parked cars; there were two others the same model and color as Vern's.

Tom drove slowly up to the door, the headlights shining on the porch at the side of the house, partially hidden by shrubs.

There were two people, close together, standing in the porch dark, just outside the doorway. The woman had both arms around the man's neck, kissing him.

Tom saw in the glare of the headlights, it was the painter lady, Maggie, and when the man turned slightly, he saw Vern, his hands up under the red sheer blouse.

Tom's mouth dropped open, and he turned to Bliss, looking at the couple intently.

Neither of them spoke.

Tom had a pang of guilt for putting the headlights on the two people, and at the same time, felt fear for what Bliss's response was going to be.

"Take me home," Bliss said, still glaring in the direction of Vern and the woman, even thought Tom had moved the car slightly, so the light beams were away from exposing the couple on the porch.

"As soon as Vern comes out," Tom said, hesitantly.

"Leave him," Bliss said coldly, looking at him.

Tom, not sure of what to do, said, "Okay," and realized, suddenly, he was now taking Bliss's side -- inadvertently.

Turning the Mercedes, driving down the sloping driveway, Tom said, "It looked to me -- she was clinging onto Vern. Maybe it was all Maggie's doing."

"Don't try to help him, Tom. You two are long-time friends, but you can't help him in this."

"He's been with other women since I was pregnant with Frederick."

"Okay, okay," Tom said. Then after a silence, he added, "I think I should go over to Kyle's house tonight -- sleep on the couch. I don't want to be around -- when Vern gets home."

Bliss was silent, so Tom did not say any more, until he stopped the big car in front of the house garage door.

"Tell Melanie I'll take her home on the motorcycle," he said to Bliss, looking at the Porsche parked off to the side of the driveway, "then I'll go over to Kyle's -- wake them up, ask if I can use their couch."

Bliss opened the car door, and getting out, looked back at Tom, saying, "How come -- you and I -- never got together?"

She stood, holding the car door open, waiting for his answer.

He thought of making a wisecrack. Something like, 'You're too expensive,' but he said, "You were always going with some guy -- when I came home from my travels."

"That's not an answer," she said, and slammed the car door.

CHAPTER 18

"You don't mind riding on a motorcycle?" Tom said, up to Melanie, as she came down the steps from the house.

He started the Bultaco, and stood astride it, holding the handlebars.

"No," She said, smiling as she walked up to him, "I dig bikes."

When she climbed on behind him, he liked feeling her hard breasts against his back, and her thighs holding his, from behind.

At the bottom of the driveway, Tom turned right on the road, going up the canyon, instead of turning left, the direction of Melanie's house.

He wanted to be alone with her.

But near the top of the steep road, he spotted a Chevrolet, parked in a dirt lane the power company uses when inspecting overhead electric wires.

Tom slowed the Bultaco, and drove closer to the parked car. When the cycle headlight flashed on the rear of the vehicle, he saw the license plate was Nevada, and there was no one inside.

If the car had out-of-state license plates, it could be a police undercover car. He knew they frequently used the trick during their work.

"What's the matter?" Melanie said. "Why are we here?"

"I'm just turning around," Tom said. "My gears are sticking -- I just ran the cycle up the hill to work them out."

The motor was running, and to put her at ease, he asked, "Hey, how did you meet your boyfriend? That Jarred guy?"

"My mom is diabetic," she said, "and I get her Insulin, and those test strips --from the drug store his dad owns."

"Is that <u>all</u> you get from the drug store?" Tom asked, grinning.

"Yeah," she said, Tom feeling her relaxing against him, "sometimes he gets stuff for me -- Codeine -- sometimes Quaaludes."

"You keep taking that stuff," Tom said, "you're going to end up in a rubber room."

"I know -- I know," she said. "Sometimes I sell it at school -- to friends -- when I need money."

"You know what will happen," Tom said, "if you get caught doing that -- don't you?"

"Yes."

"Hang on," Tom said, "we better get you home."

The prospect of the police being nearby had changed Tom's thinking about making moves on Melanie.

They roared down the hill road, back past the Hurley house, and stopped at the driveway up to Melanie's house.

"You want me to buzz you up?"

"Yeah," she said, pulling tighter against him.

The headlight caught her mother, standing on the porch in her bathrobe.

"Mom -- it's me -- Melanie," she shouted, over Tom's shoulder.

Tom saw the mother put a gun in the pocket of her robe, as he stopped the Bultaco, shut off the motor.

"I thought," the mother said, "it was those creeps again. I thought they -- came back."

"I brought her home on the motorcycle," Tom offered, weakly, "so she'd be safe."

"There were two guys in the woods -- out back -- a little while ago," the mother said calmly. "I aimed at them with my gun -- and all it did was <u>click</u>, <u>click</u>, <u>click</u> -- three times. No bullets -- the damn thing isn't even loaded."

Melanie swung off the motorcycle.

"C'mon, mom," she said. "Let's go in the house."

"You bet," Tom said, admiring her, a bright kid, who saved her mother -- and on top of everything, had looks that could charm the birds out of the trees.

Starting the Bultaco, turning it around, Tom had the sudden thought, maybe the two guys were cops, who parked the Chevy down the road.

"But what the hell," he said, "are they looking for? A prowler? Maybe. Or maybe they're <u>watching</u> -- somebody," he said, turning at the roadway at the bottom of the hill, heading for Kyle's house.

"They wouldn't be watching me," Tom said, shifting through the gears of the Bultaco, "so they must be watching Vern. But why? What the hell did he do? What's he into?"

Kyle came to the front door, looking through the screen, when he heard the Bultaco drive up.

"You know what time it is?" he said, half-whispering. "I don't care -- if you're drunk or not."

Sliding off the Bultaco, putting down the kick stand, Tom said quietly, "Bliss caught Vern playing -- kissy-face -- with a dame at the lawyer party -- up in Sausalito. I drove her home -- in the big car. We left him there."

"Oh-h, shit," Kyle said quietly.

"I didn't want to be there -- at the house -- when Vern gets home," Tom said from the bottom of the steps. "Can I sleep on your couch -- tonight?"

"Doris won't like it," Kyle said, "but come in."

He swung open the screen door.

Starting up the steps, Tom said, "I think they are headed for a divorce."

"Don't say that," Kyle said, as Tom walked past him into the house. "Don't talk like that," he snapped.

"That's terrible -- I don't like to hear stuff like that," he mumbled, closing the screen door.

"All right," Tom said, sitting down on the couch, "have it your way.

"Tomorrow," he said taking off his shoes, "I'd like to use the phone -- call home -- collect -- ask for a hundred and twenty for air fare."

"Gee-ze," Kyle said quietly. Then added, "I'll get you a pillow -- and a blanket."

"Forget it," Tom said, knowing Doris did not like him in the house. He brushed away her over-active son, once, who continually crawled up on the couch, and on his back, and Doris considered Tom a threat to the boy.

"Okay," Kyle said wearily.

*   *   *   *   *

Tom had a dream, sleeping heavily on the couch, arms folded over his chest for warmth.

He dreamed he was in the bedroom, sleeping at the Hurley house, and he woke late at night to see a figure in a white gown, open the door, come in and stand over him.

It was a woman, and Tom rose up on one elbow, to hear a <u>swish</u>, and the gown fell to the floor. The figure, lifting his covering sheet, slid into the bed next to him.

A soft hand covered his mouth, as he felt a warm fleshly body press against his side.

They made love slowly, at first, then came a muted sigh, and he began to feel moisture they were both giving off, as their breathing grew heavier, with their pushing against one another, eagerly.

Tom fought hard to hold back coming to a climax, thrusting wildly, until he was overcome, and released.

They lay for a moment, both breathing hard. Then the woman put her soft hand on his mouth again, before she slipped out of the bed, taking the gown, and going out, closing the door, silently.

*   *   *   *   *

The next morning, Saturday, Tom woke up on the couch, when he heard the Porsche engine out on the driveway of Kyle's house.

When Tom crossed to the screen door, Vern was coming up.

"Come with me to the office," he said, opening the door, taking off his shade-adjusting sunglasses, "and we can talk about the party last night. I got to talk to -- somebody."

"Like this?" Tom said. He was still wearing the pineapple shirt.

"You look okay," Vern said, swinging his sunglasses, "we'll only be at the office a few minutes."

"I'm scheduled for flight lessons today -- at the airport, you can watch me practice takeoff and landing. Okay?"

"Did you talk to Bliss?" Tom asked, looking up from sitting on the couch, putting his shoes on. "About the party?"

"No, her bedroom door was closed," he said quietly, "so I didn't press my luck. When she cools off, I'll reason with her.

"I got to explain to her -- that other women -- are part of the legal business. You got to make <u>friends</u> -- you use that kind of friendship -- to get ahead."

"Sounds like a hard case to plead," Tom said, standing up, pulling down on the pineapple shirt, feeling grubby, looking at Vern in his blue golf shirt and crisp slacks. "You got your work cut out for you."

Kyle came in from the bedroom, barefoot, wearing only Levi's.

"You guys want coffee?" he asked, not sounding like he meant it.

"No, thanks," Vern said. "We got to run -- I got a real early appointment at my office this morning."

Down in the driveway, Vern said to Tom, while opening the door of the Porsche, "I got a pint of cognac under the seat."

"That sounds like the kind of breakfast I need," Tom said, looking up at Kyle, who had followed them out.

"Thanks for letting me crash here last night, Kyle," Tom said quietly. "Keep an eye on the Bultaco for me."

"You can use the Bultaco," Vern said. "We'll be gone until after lunch."

"Okay," Kyle said, nodding. "I'll see you guys later."

When they were driving down on the road below Kyle's house, Vern reached under the seat, and with the pint of cognac, he pulled out a letter from under the seat.

"This letter for you," Vern said, "was in all the mail piled on my desk," handing it to Tom. "I don't know when it came.

"I found it, when I was going through my contract papers again, last night. It's from your girlfriend."

Tom took two drinks of the cognac and sat, holding the bottle between his knees, opening the letter from Ann.

"Wish I could have a morning snort," Vern said, "but not when -- before -- I'm going to be flying."

They were crossing the bridge from Berkeley to San Francisco, Tom reading the letter.

"Man," he said, "Ann's father is getting married again," and took another swallow of cognac. "The old fart will be moving to Charlotte, Virginia -- his new wife is a widow -- with a big house down there -- with a garden.

"He's giving Ann his old house -- she says we can make camp there -- when I get back."

"Ha," Vern said. "Now -- what are you going to do? Go back home -- or stay out here? Well -- at least you got a choice, Tom. I wish I could say the same. I'm really in the soup -- Bliss is really mad."

"Maybe," Tom said taking a sip of cognac, "she'll cool off -- you can talk to her -- persuade her that last night was just a -- fluke."

"Yeah, maybe," Vern said. "Hell, right now -- she won't even talk to me. She says she's going to hire a lawyer -- for a divorce. She says I can talk to him."

"Uh-hoo," Tom said, "that sounds serious, Vern." Tom looking at him, then turned to drink a quick cognac.

"What did Bliss say," Vern said slowly, his lawyer instinct working, "when you two drove home last night?"

"Yeah," Tom said feeling the effect of the warming cognac, "she suspects -- stuff like what went on -- on the porch -- has been going on for some time.

"She," Tom, recalling all her complaining over the last few weeks, summarizing, said, "blames all the travel you do -- that contract -- negotiation stuff."

"Aw, hell," Vern said, turning off the bridge, entering the city traffic, "I was away too much. I couldn't help it. The world is full of willing girls."

Tom sat folding the letter from Ann, feeling guilty for telling Vern Bliss's suspicions about his womanizing, and said, slowly, "It would be hard for me -- to stay in one place -- all the time."

"That's all there is, kid," Vern said, downshifting in the slowing traffic, the Porsche lurching. "You stay in one place -- and grow old."

"Yeah," Tom said, feeling light-headed from the cognac, then asked, "would you loan me a hundred and twenty bucks -- for air fare? I got to go home for a while -- things have changed. I got to talk to Ann -- and hash out what we're going to do."

"That's Fisherman's Whorf," Vern said, "over there."

"You see one whorf with fishing boats," Tom said, "you've seen them all, sluggo."

"Tom, you sound smashed."

"Cognac on an empty stomach," Tom said smiling. "It works wonders -- in a hurry. But, right now, I got to tap a kidney -- real soon."

"You can use the bathroom at my office," Vern said, grinning, "we're almost there. Hey, I want to ask you to stay in Berkeley -- talk to Bliss -- help me get her back. She listens to you -- what you say."

"So that's why you brought the cognac, you rat."

"Stay here Tom, I need your help."

"So does my bladder. It's sending me an urgent message."

"My office is just up ahead, hold on."

They drove into a concrete parking lot, three levels, and Vern's spot was near the elevator, on the second floor. They made a quick exit, only to cross the street, and enter another elevator, up to his office on the fifth floor.

"I look like I've been on a three day binge," Tom said, as they rode up in the elevator, pulling at the pineapple shirt.

"It's Saturday," Vern said grinning. "You're supposed to dress casual -- for the office."

"I'll go straight for the bathroom," Tom said, "as soon as we get to your office."

"Don't frighten Missus Tolliver, our elderly secretary."

"I'll hold everything -- until I get to the urinal."

Vern unlocked the door with a key, Tom watching, doing a dance, reading the list of lawyers on the door Vern shared office space with.

"I got to piss like a rocket," Tom said as Vern swung open the door.

Three men in dark suits, white shirts, and trim haircuts, were standing in the office near the desk.

"Vernon Bennett Hurley?" the shortest man, older than the other two, asked.

"Yes, I'm Hurley."

"We're from the Justice Department, San Francisco division, and we are arresting you on an indictment for misappropriating government funds -- namely from the Army payroll section at Fort Ord, California, during your period of military service."

Vern stood, staring at the shorter man, as he read from a clutch of papers, while the other two men held out identification cards, verifying their authority.

"Oh-h," Missus Tolliver said from her desk, "this is terrible."

Tom said, "This is crazy," before bolting into the bathroom.

"We have in the indictment," the shorter man said, continuing his reading, "that the accused, in addition to purchasing a diamond ring from the Majestic Jewelers here in San Francisco, for the sum of two-thousand, seven hundred and eighty dollars, the accused purchased nine round-trip America Airline tickets from Detroit to San Francisco, for a Bliss Ruth Caldwell of Detroit -- during the period of his Army service."

"Missus Tolliver," Vern said, "call my father's law firm in Detroit -- tell him I've been arrested for embezzlement -- and say I want him to come to San Francisco -- to aid in my legal defense."

"Yes, Mister Hurley," she said quietly.

Tom came out of the bathroom, drying his hands on the front of the pineapple shirt, and saw the two younger men, step up to either side of Vern, one saying, "Put your hands behind your back."

The other man handcuffed Vern slowly.

"What can I do, Vern?" Tom asked him.

"Tell Bliss -- and take the Porsche home."

"I don't have the keys."

"They're under the front seat."

Three of the other lawyers, who worked with Vern, came into the room from their outer offices, and stood quietly, watching Vern being lead to the door.

One of these lawyers was dressed in a yellow golf shirt and slacks; Tom, looking at them, knew they had been a part of the charade -- that brought Vern to the office on a Saturday for the arrest.

"You bastards," Tom said in a hoarse voice.

"What else could we do?" one of them asked, a bald man, his hands turned, palms up.

"Not been so willing," Tom said, hearing the door close.

Later, in the parking garage, after Tom climbed into the seat of the Porsche, he reached a hand under for the keys.

Four plastic packs of condoms slid out with the ring of keys.

Tom, looking at the packs, said, "Vern was asking for it," while shaking his head, slowly, "and he got it -- from <u>everybody</u>."

*   *   *   *

Back at the house, Tom told Bliss about Vern's arrest, as they sat at the kitchen table.

She screamed.

Then she said to Tom, "I <u>knew</u> they were watching the house for some reason. Oh-h, that does it -- he and I are done."

While she took the children to Missus Kelsey, for an overnight stay, Tom telephoned home to Detroit, asking for one hundred-twenty dollars to buy a return airline ticket.

As he stepped out of Vern's office, Bliss came in the house front door.

"Stay with me tonight," she said. "I need to <u>hold</u> someone."

"I can't do that, Bliss. He's still your husband," Tom said quietly, leaning against the office door jam.

"The best time of my life," she said, "when I was young -- it was fun coming out here to California -- to see him while he was in the Army.

"Now I find out -- the best time of our lives -- was on <u>stolen</u> <u>money</u>."

Tom looked down at his shoes, to avoid looking at her drawn face.

"Even -- even," she said biting at her lower lip, "the engagement ring money -- is tainted by theft -- stolen. Oh-h, I feel sick." She choked. "I'm leaving him."

"Let him explain," Tom said. "Give him a chance to tell his side of the story. Wait a bit -- he'll be out on bond --"

"No," she said. "Seeing him with that woman on the porch -- at that damn party -- and now this comes out, about stealing money from the Army -- it's all too much, Tom," she said wiping her face.

"I've made up my mind," she said. "I want a divorce."

Tom stood away from the door jam, looking at her, grimacing.
"I <u>want</u> you to stay here with me tonight, Tom, I'm asking you."

THE END

14 September, 2014
St. Clair Shores, Michigan

ABOUT THE AUTHOR

The author lived in Spain, Southern France and Germany, following his graduation from Wayne State University in Detroit, his hometown. A chronic illness brought him home, but soon moved to Florida, and began writing for a newspaper.

But again his illness forced him to move and he sought the dry climate of the southwest, settling in Taos, New Mexico. Then on the urging of friends, moved to Berkeley, California, where he began writing fiction, turning away from journalism.

When family matters forced him to return to Detroit, he moved back, and continued his fiction writing there.

He now lives in the family house near Lake St. Clair, and writes fiction stories for the electronic book market.